CW00521597

Red Shoes
And
Other Short Stories

By Janet Pywell

Red Shoes and Other Short Stories

This is a work of fiction. All names, characters, and incidents are the product of the author's imagination. Any resemblance to real persons, living or dead, is entirely coincidental.

Copyright © 2013 Janet Pywell. All rights reserved.

The right of Janet Pywell to be identified as the author of this work has been asserted by her in accordance with the Copyright, Designs and Patents Act 1988. A CIP catalogue record for this book is available from the British Library.
No part of this publication may be reproduced, stored in a retrieval system, or transmitted in any other way by any means without the prior permission of the copyright holder, except as provided by USA copyright law.

ISBN: 978-0-9926686-3-1

Cover Art copyright © 2013 Book Graphics

Author's cover picture by Mark Barton, Parkway Photography
Published by Richmond Heights Publishing

For more information visit:
www.janetpywell.com
blog: janetpywell.wordpress.com

For Veronica
With Love
All short stories tell another story…

My grateful thanks and appreciation to my wonderful family for all their support, understanding, humour and kindness in helping me complete this book of short stories.

Once again, this book would never have been completed without the advice and support from my friend and mentor, fellow Irish author Joe McCoubrey, whose commitment and guidance in this marathon has kept me focused.

A note from the Author

I have read numerous books of short stories and, in my experience, they normally contain a theme or a thread connecting them. Let me assure you that with Red Shoes and Other Short Stories this is not the case. This is an eclectic mix of tales. All stand-alone stories that I hope you will dip in and dip out of, as your mood takes you.

Some of these stories are based on fact. For example, on April 7th, 1943 an American Flying Fortress called T'aint a bird was en route from Africa to England when it ran out of fuel. It strayed off course, and eventually landed near Clonakilty and the island of Inchydoney. There was a crew of ten, an eleventh mystery passenger, and a pet monkey who were all uninjured. They were interned for three days by the Irish Local Defence Force at O'Donovan's Hotel and reports at the time described the event saying, 'a carnival atmosphere ensured in war-time rationed Clonakilty.'

Conchita Cintron, a Peruvian torera (a female bullfighter) was probably the most famous in the history of bullfighting. The final corrida of the 1949 season, in Jaén, Spain, was to be the last of her career but she did enter the ring one more time in 1950. Conchita went on to marry a Portuguese nobleman and nephew of her teacher, Ruy da Cámara. They lived in Portugal and had six children.

Sarah Ponsonby and Eleanor Butler, two Irish upper-class women, whose relationship outraged family and enchanted friends, eloped to live in Plas Newydd. They became the Ladies of Llangollen, and their home, a haven to writers such as; Wordsworth, Shelley and Byron. They are buried together in St Collen's church in Llangollen, Wales.

Stari Most is a reconstruction of a 16th-century Ottoman bridge in the city of Mostar. It crosses the river Neretva and connects two parts of the city. The original Old Bridge was destroyed in November 1993 by Bosnian Croat forces during the Croat-Bosniak War. The rebuilt bridge opened in July 2004. It is still used by young boys to show off their diving skills. For anyone who has travelled to this area, they will know of the scars and sadness that underline the beauty of this special country.

If you read and enjoyed my novel The Golden Icon then you may be interested in Dublin 1832 - the prelude to the novel. Glasnevin Cemetery was known as Prospect Cemetery and is the resting place for Protestants and Catholics and other religious orders. It contains the graves of many of Ireland's most prolific national figures; from literary writers to philanthropists and politicians. It also holds an interesting and historical variety of grave monuments from the austere to the more elaborate Celtic crosses.

And as for Red Shoes…do we truly know our neighbours?

Table of Contents

Red Shoes

Harry waves at me from across the road. He is standing beside his shiny white Mercedes.

I ignore him, open the back door of my old Vauxhall and Matt and Jason tumble out like floppy dolls.

"Jo! I've got the newspaper." He crosses the suburban road that divides us. "There's a company advertising that creates websites. Are you still going ahead with your homemade jewellery?" He whacks the rolled-up paper against his palm and then ruffles his son's hair. "Hi Jason."

I stare at the birthmark on his cheek. It's like a giant tear drop.

"There are also a few jobs in here, insurance, sales, care workers or you could train as a beauty consultant," he lowers his voice. "I know things aren't easy."

I don't tell him things are worse and that Gary has been made redundant and has stopped my payments.

I watch the boys pull their school bags from the back seat, a crumpled crisp bag falls to the floor and Matt stuffs it in his pocket.

I collected the boys from their swimming class. We are neighbours, and the boys are in the same year at school, so Harry and I take it in turns to fetch and carry.

"Dad?" Jason grabs Harry's arm. "Mr Rogers

1

wants to take us on a trip next month, rock climbing and canoeing, can I go? The whole class is going."

Matt is scuffing his shoes on the cement. His blond hair is getting curlier and it sits on the collar of this school shirt. He doesn't look up at me.

"Mr Rogers says it's educational." Jason has his father's sleepy brown eyes.

"Sounds exciting." Harry tries to make meaningful eye contact with me. "The new Head seems to be having a positive effect on the school." He winks and the tear drop disappears into the folds of skin under his eye.

I lift a shopping bag from the boot, we say goodbye and I take Matt inside the house.

After dinner and his bath, I'm stuffing his Transformers into a cupboard when he grabs Dark of the Moon and hugs it against his chest. He curls up like an unhappy question mark on top of his Star Wars duvet and watches me as I stack his Horrid Henry books under the bed. His bottom lip pouts out, his shiny button eyes are close to tears and his nose turns pink.

"I can't go on the school trip, can I?"

"We'll see."

My break up with Gary wasn't easy. But Matt is more settled and happy in the past few months than he's been in a long time. I know I must thank the new Head, Mr Rogers, for taking an interest in Matt, but I haven't been inside the school since Gary left.

"Are we poor?" Matt asks.

"No! There's plenty worse off than us." I kneel on the floor and pull his hands together in mine.

"Can't Daddy give us more money?"

"No sweetheart, he's got his new family to look after. Now, it's time to sleep."

His eyes well up with tears. "I'm not in the school play," he says. "Mr Rogers says I may be in the one at Christmas."

"Mr Rogers sounds very sensible." I squeeze his fingers.

"Story?" Matt grabs Horrid Henry. His reading has improved in the past few months, it passes twenty minutes, and when I see his eyes turn drowsy and his thick eyelashes close I slide the book from his fingers and kiss his soft cheek.

I reach for the light switch.

"I like your new red shoes," his sleepy voice makes me pause and I wait just long enough to know he's fallen asleep and I leave the door ajar.

In the kitchen I pour a glass of white wine and dial the familiar number. It clicks to answer phone, the same as it did yesterday, and the day before that.

"Gary, pick up the phone! We may not be married any more but at least you could answer my calls."

I take a slug of wine, pick up the shopping bag and open the box. My new patent-red shoes twinkle back at me. I take my time twisting them in my hand, admiring their shape, inhaling the leather and stroking the ridiculously high heels.

I'll have to be careful not to fall.

The phone interrupts my daydreaming. It's Jackie, one of the models I've worked with a few times before I was made redundant at the Fashion Academy. She always says my designs are world-class and I always reply, it's a shame the Director didn't think so.

We chat and she asks me questions. Have I found a job? - no. How's Matt? - fine. Love life? - stagnant.

Then she tells me they are all going abroad for a long weekend.

"It's Sophie's hen-party. It won't cost a lot. Four days in Madrid: shopping, drinking and hopefully some rampant sex with a local," she laughs and adds, "for me, not for Sophie."

At her insistence I promise her I'll think about it.

When I hang up, I top up my wine glass and gaze at the jewellery I've laid out on the kitchen table: necklaces, bracelets, beads and a few rings that I've bashed into shape. They are all bits I've picked up in second-hand shops, colourful stones and antique chains. All unusual pieces that I'm cleaning, remodelling and reshaping. It's time-consuming and so far it hasn't been profitable. Under a stack of papers I see the envelope that haunts me. I open it again and reread the statement. It's not good news. The bank wants its money back.

I pick up my sparkling red shoes and armed with my wine glass I tread quietly upstairs. In the bathroom, I wipe the mirror with a tissue and check my reflection. With shaking hands I use heavy foundation to cover the circles under my eyes and spots on my chin. I add pink lipstick and smile, revealing a gap between my front teeth. I'm a natural blond. My hair is long and I tease it into shape with hot tongs before flicking it over my left shoulder and striking a sideways pose. It's one I've been practising for a few weeks. I blow myself a kiss.

With a small sigh I strip naked and dress

carefully in new lace underwear and cover myself in a Japanese-style kimono painted with gaudy exotic birds.

I shiver. Has the heating gone off?

The doorbell rings.

I trail my hand along the banister and walk downstairs. My palms are sticky and it's hard to open the front door. The round handle slips in my grasp and I tug back the bolt.

On the doorstep Harry, who has changed from his work-suit into blue jeans and a cashmere sweater, is breathless and excited.

"I forgot to tell you," he says. "They're opening a new supermarket and they want shelf-stackers. It might be a foot in the door for you...Jo? Are you going out?" He frowns, his eyes turn down and his birthmark changes into an elongated island.

I tug my kimono tighter at the neck. "No..."

"You look, well, you look…have you got makeup on? Is…is someone coming round?"

"Have you left Jason at home alone?"

"Yes, but–"

"I'll see you tomorrow, Harry." I begin to close the door.

"I only want to help–"

The window rattles as the door slams and the reverberation thumps in tune with my banging heart, and beating butterfly wings that are somersaulting in my stomach.

Back upstairs, I cover my double bed with pink satin sheets and matching pillow cases with silver hearts. I take a fake mink coat and a leather jacket from my wardrobe and drape them over a chair. I leave high heel black boots in a corner and arrange a few clothes over the end of the bed: white blouse, school tie, school skirt and a silky pink nightdress.

It's what the handy guide says to do.

I trace the cracked lid of my laptop and place it on a small table, press the button and it burrs into life. While I wait I scan the check list. It's like a contract. I've agreed to fulfil fantasies: strip, dance and dress-up but I said no to inserting objects inside, masturbation or talking dirty. My throat feels dry and my fingers are shaking.

I type in: Livejasmin.com.

I have my own login and password and 'they' control the minutes I work. I get one pound seventy-five per minute and viewers are entitled to one free minute. They can watch me before they decide to buy my time. It's what the guide says.

I think about Jackie and how she struts on the catwalk, so I stroll slowly around the bed thrusting out my hips but I feel stupid and I sit on the mattress. My toe nails need cutting and I pick at a jagged edge until it feels smoother. I can't go and get nail scissors now. I'm supposed to be working.

I pick up a magazine and lay diagonally across the sheets bunching the silver hearts against my small breasts trying to make my cleavage look as alluring as the Grand Canyon but they are as inviting as mole hills.

I don't want to reveal too much. They can pay for that.

The advice in the handy guide says, smile, you are somebody's fantasy, so I say it aloud and my voice echoes and sounds hollow in the empty room. I put on gaudy jewellery: bangles, rings, and imitation pearls and leap back onto the bed. I am in direct line with the eye of the camera when a pop-up appears.

Each individual guest to the website has their own unique number.

Several guests send text messages on the screen. Some are in a language I don't understand.

I try smiling. I want to be somebody's fantasy, someone's dream.

Guest 528 writes that he wants me to take off my kimono, another wants to see my body, one wants to see my neck.

I have a minute to tempt them so I pout, flick my hair and blow a kiss. Very slowly I shake my curls over my shoulder trying to be seductive but I feel silly.

Once a Guest is paying – the handy guide says – do as they ask.

Guest 534 is paying so I pose provocatively as I've seen Jackie do, and drape my kimono down my back and across my arm.

One pound seventy-five per minute. I go very, very slowly.

What boots have you got? He types.

I can't see him but I assume he's male.

It doesn't take me long to pull them on and zip them up. Afterwards he wants fluffy slippers, high heels, flip flops, Ugg boots and finally I slide into my new red shoes.

He asks me to lie on my back, on the bed. He asks me to rub the heel of the shoe against my calf then he tells me to take them off. He wants me to wriggle my toes and he texts that he would like to kiss them.

I giggle.

Then Guest 534 is gone. The screen is blank.

I sit up then potter around the bedroom. I straighten the sheets and make sure the curtains are pulled tight but not before I peak outside. Harry's bedroom light is on, like me, he sleeps at the front of the house.

The computer bings.

Guest 576.

Are you spying on your neighbours?

I shake my head and smile. He can't hear me. I lie back on the bed, tilting my head, so my hair falls partly across my face.

You can be my next door neighbour, he types. Would you like that?

I nod.

What would you do for me?

I bite my lip. I try Jackie's model smile but my face feels distorted. I must look ridiculous. I try to be innocent and make my eyes big and wide like the typical girl next door but then an image of Harry's face comes into my vision… and then my other neighbours…. Oh my God! What if they knew what I was doing? My stomach shifts uncomfortably and I turn to look over my shoulder. The curtains are drawn tight but unease festers and flutters inside me.

I look back at the screen.

Are you nervous?

Yes – but I shake my head.

Suck your finger.

I flick the switch and Guest 576 is gone.

My breathing is working as fast as my mind. I'm

dizzy and feel sick.

What would be the odds of me knowing someone? I take deep calming breaths. It's impossible. It's my imagination. I think of Matt's smiling face and how much he wants to go on the school trip. Matt is happier and gaining confidence at school thanks to Mr Rogers, and then I think of Jackie and Sophie and the hen-weekend in Madrid, and I sigh aloud. I think of having fun, going out for dinner and feeling good, and I think of Christmas looming and the bank's letter on the table in the kitchen.

The screen comes to life again.

I forget they can still see me.

Guest 865 - You look thoughtful.

Thank goodness I don't have to speak. My mouth is dry.

Guest 873 joins in – Thinking of me baby?

Some have codenames like Menphis, Happyone and Boredman, and there are foreigners with name like Mikael, Slav, Ismael.

I am shocked when they write what they would like to do to me but I smile.

Flirtyman types. Make the screen two-way—I want u to c me.

He's paying.

The handy guide says this is good. It means I can slow down my performance according to his needs and I can earn more money. He wants to see my underwear and he asks me to strip very slowly. I smile conscious of the gap in my teeth and I begin counting the minutes.

Several more guests, and a few hours later, I hear a noise on the landing.

I tie my kimono at the waist and unlock the bedroom door.

Matt is on his way back from the bathroom. He walks rubbing his eyes with his fist and climbs back into bed. I follow him, pull the duvet round his shoulders and kiss his forehead. He takes the silky sleeve of my gown and rubs it against his cheek. His voice is soft.

"Why are you wearing your red shoes?"

***

By the end of November I have established a routine. I work at night and I have a day-time schedule. At 3pm it's slow for internet sex which means I collect Matt from school. Jason has football practise so Harry will collect him later.

Today the wind has whipped my hair around my face causing my eyes to sting and tears to fall down my cheeks. I wipe them with the back of my hand, hug my coat around my waist and cross the deserted playground.

Mr Rogers is standing in the doorway. I'm surprised to see how young he is, but with foppish hair, square glasses and a blue bow tie, I think him old-fashioned and dated.

He blushes when I flick my hair over my shoulder and smile. His grey eyes are serious when he tells me he's pleased with Matt's increasing confidence. That is when he smiles and the sides of his mouth go down like a clown and I see he has dimples in each cheek.

"Matt's thrilled he's in the nativity play this

year," I reply.

"He deserves to be." Mr Rogers ruffles Matt's hair. "He has a lovely voice and he's turning out to be a good shepherd."

For the first time Matt doesn't take my hand as we walk away. Instead he shoves them firmly in his pockets and begins humming a familiar carol.

Tonight Harry and Jason are eating dinner with us. In the past month, I've been on a few dates with Harry. He's very persistent. He's even helped me set up my jewellery business online. It's not making much money but I lie and tell him Gary is making his payments. He's seen my recently purchased, powder-blue, BMW parked in the driveway. I don't have the heart to tell him there is no money in second-hand trinkets.

I am at the cooker stirring the casserole when Harry leans to whisper in my ear. The boys who are at the table, nudge each other, make slurping noises and groan aloud.

"I've booked a table in The Guinea Pig for Friday night," he says. "Will you have dinner with me? There's something I want to ask you." He takes my hand and kisses the third finger on my left hand. His birthmark forms the shape of a rounded Gourd.

Matt begins singing, "Away in a Manger…" His voice is high and soft and he hums, "lays down his sweet head…"

He's practicing, and Jason who is Joseph in the nativity play begins pulling faces, giggling and trying to distract him.

They loved their school trip, rock climbing and canoeing, and they are now into the rugby season. I am grateful Mr Rogers has told Matt he is a natural player.

I push brochures for USA aside, place the steaming pot on the table, add jacket potatoes in tin foil and sit down.

I went to Madrid on the hen-weekend with the girls and in the New Year we're going to New York. Jackie is intent on having sex again with a local. I slide the brochure away from Harry's watchful gaze.

Later that evening, after Harry and Jason have gone home and Matt is in bed, I go to work. I haven't told anyone about my real job, although I've met many girls on the internet in my line of work.

My new friend Ruby from Dublin phones and tells me there's more money in films.

"Almost five euro a minute," she says. "Last month I earned over two hundred euro an hour."

She's twenty-four, has a degree in marketing and has bought her own home.

"You need to build your own fan base," she says to me. "You need to direct them to a pay-per-view personalised branded website. You can buy software linking to internet dating sites and when a bloke can't find a partner they get a surge of popup links to view other girls on live webcams. That's how you get them..."

I mumble that I'm not sure and I'd need to work on my website skills.

I think about the regular clients I've developed. Joshua likes to see my face when I rub a balloon over my skin. I flick on the microphone and he can hear the noise of the rubber against my body too.

Dieter likes to talk about what he wants to do to

me, which isn't very flattering and I'm thankful that he isn't a boyfriend.

And Jamal has almond-shaped eyes. He likes me to watch him dress as a woman and I give him tips on how to look more feminine. He's more beautiful than many models I dressed when I worked in the fashion industry. I think if ever went back into that business I'd create a range for transsexuals and cross-dressers.

My clients are varied. I've even had a few women but I'm lucky there haven't been more weirdoes. Basically I realise people are lonely. They want company or a smile from a pretty face or something they don't get in their own homes or from their partners. They want excitement, teasing, stimulation or simply just someone to talk to.

"You should start a new website," Ruby advises. "Do you know there's a demand for fat-arsed girls?" she says before hanging up.

I'm thinking about Ruby, websites and films and two hundred Euro an hour when Guest 1286 pops up.

Modestman.

He's my nineteenth tonight and I'm ready to sleep but I lean back on the bed, put on my red shoes and smile seductively. Sometimes it's hard to keep the smile on my face, but it must be the same in any job, air hostess, public relations, sales, after all it's just a job.

Modestman asks me to make the camera two-way. He's a regular. He's probably been on fifteen times in the past month but I've never seen his face and so I flick the switch without an ounce of interest or curiosity.

My mouth dries. Blood rushes to my head and I

think I'm going to pass out.

I open my mouth and oddly, I can see my face reflected back in the screen.

My eyes are wide in shock and my gapped-tooth smile is frozen.

Behind my superimposed face is another face.

This time there's no bow tie or square glasses only the foppish hair, the down-turned smile and Mr Rogers's dimples.

T'aint a Bird

The boys' faces were huge and out of proportion as they leaned over him.

"Ya a feckin' looser!" one said.

"Suck it, ya eejit!"

"Puff on it!"

Kieran O'Sullivan felt sick. He was pushed up against the wall sitting in a puddle. His trousers were wet. Cigar smoke on the back of his throat made him choke.

"Ya wee shite!" said the oldest bully, grabbing his throat. "Eejit! Eejit! Eejit!"

His eyes watered. The chanting of their voices got louder and louder, becoming a heavy drone causing a throbbing in his ears. He raised his arm at the thundering noise that grew louder and louder. Then, in the sky, engines roared and a large shadow loomed out of the clouds blocking the light in the alleyway. The noise was deafening as it passed overhead.

The bullies stopped and looked up.

"Wha' the feck…?"

"Look!"

"A plane!"

"Tis gonna hit the houses…"

"Gonna crash!"

As the older boy lost the grip on his collar, Kieran pushed him out of his way and made a run for it. Dashing from the alley he caught a glimpse of an aircraft disappearing over the school roof. His heart hammered. The fear of the boys and the excitement of the plane propelled his legs into a run. He pushed passed school bins at the back of the kitchen where the scent of lunchtime cabbage soup caught in his nostrils. He jumped over potholes in the lumpy pitches of the school playing field, his arms pumping, knees shaking, past the rattling windows of the girls' school where surprised faces were pressed against the glass.

They were all staring up at the sky.

His breath came in rapid short bursts. He ran hard, stumbling, as he headed away from the town toward the marshes. At the top of the small knoll he missed his footing and dropped to his knees panting heavily. His trousers were muddied, his boots soiled and his arse damp. He'd feel the sting of his ma's anger when he got home.

The whine of the engine in the sky caused him to gasp. The plane's wing was tilting in a steep turn over the town breaking the stillness of Clonakilty's normal tranquil air. The earlier rain storm had passed and now one of the engines spluttered and coughed heavily, leaving a trail of dark smoke against white bulbous clouds.

"It's gonna stall!" he shouted.

His Uncle regularly sent him the Aeroplane magazine from America so Kieran knew it was a B-17.

The aircraft circled with a heavy growl. It was heading for White's Marsh, and in one movement, with his head held low, Kieran was up and running.

Donal Collins threw down his scythe. He was working at the edge of the field beside the flat marshlands as the plane loomed toward him. He covered his head with his arms. It skimmed the trees and forced him to his knees. The sound was thunderous. The giant wingspan blocked a momentary flash of April sun between ominous dark clouds.

The ground vibrated, shaking with uncertainty at his feet and the noise engulfed his senses.

Kieran ran toward Donal across the field, shouting and pointing, his voice lost in the aircraft's roar.

They waited in a brief moment of expectation and silent contemplation, save for Kieran's ragged breathing.

"Ain't that a sight?" Donal stood up flicking mud from his arms, not taking his eyes from the plane. "They're lucky finding the marsh."

"They're Yanks! Tis a flying fortress, Donal."

"Well, t'ain't a bird, is it lad?"

Kieran's eleven year-old grin was famous for its chipped tooth, the result of an adventure last year involving a pony, gunpowder and the bullying boys at school.

The plane's four engines had spluttered to a silence and it sat immobile, a giant iron bird in the middle of the wetland, out of place and uncomfortable.

A flock of shocked curlews chortled and took flight.

"Let's go! Come on!"

Donal called out, "Kieran! Wait! We don't know

17

who they are."

He felt a restraining hand on his shoulder.

The plane's hatch opened. A man's legs dangled before he dropped to the ground. He was lanky with brown curly hair. He reached into his jacket and pulled a revolver from his pocket.

"Do you speak English?" he called.

"Carse we do, ya eejit!" Kieran replied.

"Where are we?"

It was Donal who bellowed back. "Ya in White's Marsh."

"What? Where?"

"Ya in Ireland, Mister," shouted Kieran.

The man hesitated and then laughed.

He looked up at the cockpit, raised a thumb to the pilot and pocketed his gun.

Kieran watched as, one by one, the men dangled from the belly of the plane, tumbling from the aircraft and landing on the marsh. They stretched their muscles, laughed and began back-slapping each other with happy relief.

Donal took long strides across the marsh, his hand outstretched in greeting, a smile on his face.

Kieran followed, but in his excitement, he didn't notice the boggy patch and he stumbled, catching his foot in a marshy puddle. His boot filled with muddy water and he ripped a hole in the knee of his trousers.

"Shite!" He began wiping his boot on the grass. His sock was soaking. He looked up to catch the first man's salute.

"Sergeant Rice, Sir," said the man with the brown curly hair and sparkling eyes.

Donal shook his hand.

"So, we're in Ireland?" he drawled.

"Clonakilty, t'be exact. County Cork."

Kieran looked at them, his mouth open, his eyes wide. They were laughing and all talking at once with their strange accents. It was like being in the movies, only this was in colour and this was real life. They all wore green uniforms and short leather bomber jackets zipped at the front, and had wide smiles and big white teeth.

"We're on our way back from Morocco - Marrakech - we got lost in the fog! Thought we had landed in Denmark…" This one sounded like Elvis. His hair was slicked back and he stood hands on hips.

"We thought we had landed in German territory…" said another.

He strung out, terr-i-torry, and Kieran found himself repeating it in his head.

"We were s'possed t' have landed in England…."

"Got lost in the fog…" confirmed Sergeant Rice, shaking his head and contemplating the heavy clouds.

They all gathered under the wing of the aircraft until the final crewman dropped down from the hatch. He was the only one wearing a cap with a gold crest and eagle.

"Lieutenant Rowmowski," he grinned, and shook Donal's hand.

Kieran stood tall and saluted, just as he had seen the men in his Airplane magazine do, and the Lieutenant returned his salute.

"Ya da pilot?" Kieran beamed his chipped smile

"I sure am." He ruffled Kieran's hair.

Suddenly, there was scuffling and a squeal from

the hatch of the plane, a monkey leaped down and scampered onto the shoulder of the Lieutenant.

Kieran blinked.

The monkey was black and white with big dark eyes and a long tail. He looked at Kieran and began chattering loudly and baring his teeth.

Kieran's mouth fell open.

Lieutenant Rowmowski gave a deep-throated laugh and revealed a row of white teeth, not unlike the piano keys in O'Donovan's Hotel.

"Ye ain't never seen a monkey, kid?"

Kieran's feet were stuck in the mud. All eyes were on him. He shook his head and flushed red.

"Ya more interested in the plane, ain't ya?" He felt Donal's hand reassuringly on his shoulder.

Kieran nodded but he didn't take his eyes off the monkey.

"D'ye wanna touch him?" The Lieutenant smiled.

"Is he ya mascot?" Kieran knew things about the air force.

"Yup, his name's Tojo."

"Smelly little critter," said one of the airmen, causing a ripple of laughter.

"He had a red jacket and a hat when I swapped him for a carton of Lucky Strikes in Morocco," said the Lieutenant.

"He'll need clothes here," Kieran replied. "He wouldn't wanna catch cold."

The Lieutenant reached into his pocket and gave Tojo a banana. He screeched, peeling it with precision before nibbling quickly.

Kieran couldn't believe it. His ma certainly

wouldn't believe him; a banana and a monkey.

Donal nodded at the group appearing on the horizon.

"That'll be the Local Defence Force,' he said.

Two uniformed men were on a bicycle and a third rode a pony and trap.

"They'd have seen you comin' in from across the sea and circling over the town. Can't use cars. There's no petrol." He scratched the stubble on his chin. "Rationing," he added in explanation.

Tojo leaped into the air and landed on Kieran's shoulder where he began picking though his scalp. Startled, Kieran hunched his shoulders aware of its smelly breath. He'd be in serious trouble with ma if his jumper got ruined.

The LDF were followed by the important people; Donovan from the local Hotel, Doctor McMullan, and Kieran recognised the white head of hair belonging to Father Flynn, and with them were the rest of the Clonakilty town folk.

There was handshaking, laughing and banter but only Garda Coonan seemed to be taking matters seriously and he tried to put some formality to the proceedings.

To Kieran's surprise he saw his older sister Ruthie amongst the crowd. She worked in O'Donovan's Hotel. Her face was flushed red and she was smiling at Sergeant Rice. Kieran thought she looked silly pushing her hair behind her ears. He had only ever seen Ruthie this excited when she was walking out with Eddie.

"You gettin' attached to that smelly critter?" Sergeant Rice asked.

Kieran nodded.

Tojo pushed down on top of his head, his teeth chattering in imaginary conversation, biting at the collar of his shirt.

"Don't let that dirty animal mess ya up or ma'll wallop ya," Ruthie shouted. She was often short with Kieran but now he was embarrassed. He was with his new American friend, and besides, it was Kieran who had met the Yanks first.

"He ain't dirty. Besides your boyfriend Eddie would like him."

Ruthie's face clouded over, her smile faded and her eyes narrowed.

Kieran grinned back but his triumph was short-lived and his smile faded. The bullies from school stood at the edge of the crowd. They were pointing at the plane and Tojo but they glared at Kieran.

The meanest one smiled. His fist was clenched but then he opened his hand and in his palm he held the unfinished cigar. He pointed at Kieran and drew his other finger across his neck as if slitting his throat.

Tojo chattered on his shoulder and Kieran moved closer to Lieutenant Rowmowski and stood proudly beside Garda Coonan as if he were part of the important group.

The adults were discussing what to do with the airmen. Garda Coonan tried to take charge, insisting they all go to the station. He must take their details and sign forms, but Donal was unwilling to be pushed out of the limelight so quickly.

"I think we need to show these boys true Irish hospitality and give them a pint of the black stuff first…"

"Down at O'Donovan's," agreed Father Flynn quickly.

"Or something stronger," drawled the Lieutenant.

"Rationing..." Doctor McMullan looked glum.

The Lieutenant smiled and nodded at his crew. "I reckon we might have a solution for that. We stocked up before we left - come on lads, let's give these people a treat!" he shouted to his crew.

Within minutes crates of Rum and fresh fruit were being handed down from the belly of the plane and loaded onto the pony and trap. Kieran stood close to the aircraft hoping to hop onboard. He was amazed at the juicy oranges, ripe bananas and brown dates the size of pennies. They looked so tempting he wanted to grab one.

"The Lord shall provide." Father Flynn rubbed his hands in appreciation

"Tomorrow, kid," said the Lieutenant placing his cap on Kieran's head. "Once we got the papers sorted, you can sit in the cockpit."

As they began the walk to town, Kieran blended into the groups of adults and foreign airmen, avoiding Ruthie and the bullies who trailed close behind.

The crowd stopped first at the Garda station and while the airmen went inside Father Flynn rounded up the truant boys and sent them back to school.

Kieran hid behind a wall. He watched and waited until the airmen were taken to O'Donovan's Hotel. He followed them and crouched in the alleyway at the back of the hotel, near the kitchen. He settled behind the bins with Tojo who was subdued now all the fuss had died down. He was shaking with cold so Kieran removed his sweater and wrapped him in it.

After a few minutes, the Lieutenant came outside and gave him a bar of American chocolate. Kieran licked it slowly and it melted, giving him sticky fingers and when he gave a piece to Tojo, a brown mess smudged down the front of his school shirt.

In a gesture of kindness Ruthie brought him a cup of tea.

"He ain't well." Kieran lifted Tojo in his arms for them both to see.

"No, he don't look so good," agreed the Lieutenant.

"Neither do you, Kieran O'Sullivan," Ruthie said. "Look at the mess of ya, ma's gonna go thro' ya."

Kieran waited. The pub door was open. He heard Father Flynn's fiddle from inside and he tapped his foot in rhythm as he unwrapped the last chocolate square with slow and methodical delight. Tomorrow the Lieutenant had promised he could wear his cap. He would sit in the cockpit and Sergeant Rice said he would let him sit up in his gunner's position too. He could imagine firing the gun; rat-a-tat-rat-a-tat. He was going to join the Air Force. He saw himself in a pilot's uniform. The crew would stand to attention and salute him.

He dropped the last square into his mouth relishing the sticky flavour and sucked it though his chipped tooth.

The hand came out of nowhere grabbing Kieran by the throat and he spluttered melted chocolate down his chin.

"Mixin' with them Yanks! Tink ya too good

f'us?" The fingers held him firm.

"Ya gonna finish this, ya feckin' looser."

A flash of sulphur exploded near Kieran's eye. Startled Tojo leaped out of the jumper and onto the bins screeching and chattering.

"Feckin' monkey," the older boy said. "You're next!"

Kieran's stomach churned at the pungent aroma of the cigar.

"Suck on it. Ya feckin' eejit."

He shoved the cigar in Kieran's mouth.

Kieran squinted. Smoke stung his eyes. He began coughing and gagging.

Behind the boys Tojo was peering out from behind a bin. He leapt onto Kieran's shoulder and in one quick movement he moved his pelvis forward and shot a warm stream of urine all over the older bully's face.

The hand let go and the cigar fell from Kieran's mouth.

The other boys burst into laughter, pointing and clapping in delight at the older bully's discomfort.

Tojo screeched, chattering in delight, as the older boy spun away spitting and wiping his face. The boys followed the bully into the main street laughing, chanting and taunting.

"He pissed on ya."

"Ya stink like a monkey," said another.

"Stinka! Stinka!"

Kieran stood up straight, hugging Tojo in his soiled jumper, oblivious of the wrath of his ma's temper, that lay ahead.

"Who's the feckin' looser, now?" he shouted, his

voice echoing powerfully, reverberating against the alley walls and he whooped in delight. "Ya wee shite."

The Path of Darkness

Luiza's body tensed and she bit her lip as Cecilia hurled herself through the farmhouse door, slamming it against the wall, making the crockery rattle. As usual her sister's mood was combustible and their father, who sat at the head of the kitchen table, was in a similar mood.

"Shush!" Jorge Dejardim shouted. "Your mother's resting." He lifted his vest and scratched his hairy belly. A rolled-up cigarette dangled from his lips. "Give her some peace! It's about time you were home. Go and collect the eggs!"

"Why haven't you done it?"

"Don't start, or you'll know about it." Jorge raised his fist and for a few tense seconds Cecilia's muddy brown eyes out-stared him.

"I'll help you." Luiza Dejardim had been peeling potatoes. She lay down the sharp knife and grabbed a small basket. She negotiated the dark space from the table to the door with ease and familiarity. Although she had been born blind she recognised blurred shades of light but she relied upon feelings, atmosphere and emotions to guide her.

During the twenty-two years of her life she had learned to gather sounds and senses around her, imagining pictures, that she assembled like crooked jigsaw pieces. Her body was an intricately wired conduit of intuition and sensitive nerve endings. Her fingertips were her sensors, her nostrils her instinct, and her mind her compass.

She extended her hand to her young sister and breathed with reassurance as they stepped outside, away from the stale odour of the kitchen, and their father's temper.

Her head began reeling from the warm spring sunlight that tickled her cheeks. The farmhouse was perched on the hills in the Algarve and below them the fragrance of the sea, a few hundred metres away, made her lips salty.

To her right, there was a low throbbing of a fishing boat heading to the port and the odour of grilled fish wafting up from the restaurant on the beach, made her stomach rumble.

"He's lazy," Cecilia complained, dragging Luiza across the rutted field. "He does nothing. I hate him!" Her voice faded in and out against the trucks and diggers that were roaring and bleeping as they reversed on the building site in the next valley.

Fleetingly, Luiza remembered a few months ago, how Cecilia had described the luxury apartments that were being built to accommodate wealthy foreigners and Lisbonese who escaped from their busy lives to visit the coast.

"Isn't it enough that I spend the day cleaning filthy hotel rooms to pay for his beer and his tobacco? He won't even get a job. He's full of excuses!" Cecilia let go of her sister's arm.

The chickens clucked protectively as she pulled aside the mesh, reached for the eggs and placed them gently in the tattered wicker basket on Luiza's arm.

"If he sold the farm we could move somewhere comfortable and Mama would get well again. You could return to the hospital. There must be something they could do for you now. Medicine has progressed. If you saw a specialist..."

Luiza turned away. "He says the land will go up in value once the recession is over and it's best to wait." Her voice was husky as it balanced on the evening breeze.

"He's greedy! Prices are dropping every day. It'll be worth nothing by the time he sells." Cecilia pushed aside a clacking hen. "Besides, think how upset Granddad would be, if he were still alive, and saw the state of the farm. He does nothing on it!"

"Papa says there's no money in farming."

"How would he know? He's never bothered to work on it," Cecilia retorted. "Mama is depressed because we can barely pay the bills, and it's because he doesn't do anything. We live in poverty, Luiza!" In her frustration, Cecilia narrowly missed smashing an egg.

"I wish she would sing again," Luiza replied. "She always feels better when she sings in the taverna." She held her hand against the wind billowing her skirt and pulled strands of dark hair from her face, staring into her misted darkness, sensing her sister's anger and frustration.

"You have sung more in the past year than she has. All he wants to do is drink! She won't sing tonight either so you will have to go again to the taverna..."

"Will you come with me?"

Cecilia looked at her elder sister and not for the first time, she was struck by her composed serenity, and her isolation from the world. She was also aware that Luiza's voice had matured and developed into a quality beyond that of even their mother. It held a tone and resonance that stirred her senses and it was only when she heard her sister sing did she feel a sense of calm and inner peace. But, she also knew on a practical level that, had it not been for Luiza singing in the taverna, they would not be able to pay the bills.

"Of course I will, Luiza. I wouldn't let you go alone." She looked across the cliff top toward the shimmering sea. It was like an artist's blue backdrop with wispy white streaks of fine cloud, painted with a stunted brush, blending into a dusky horizon.

She sighed. She didn't know what to do any more. She had run out of ideas. Any hope that remained was draining from her, ebbing like a strong backwash, tearing and tugging the optimism from her, dragging her backward and against her will, into the depths of the sea.

As if sensing her despair, Luiza placed her slim fingers on her bare arm and began humming a mournful Portuguese folksong, and as Cecilia listened to the undulating softness that gathered around her, she was pleased Luiza couldn't see the tears gathering in her eyes.

*****

Luiza kneeled as she always did at the small shrine in the cobbled street opposite the butcher shop and beside the bakery.

Tonight, as always, she traced the outline of the Virgin Mary with the tip of her finger and felt the waxy texture of the worn statue. She imagined the gentle contours of a face she had never seen, and understood the inner self-restraint that this woman must have felt.

She remembered how, as a baby, her mother's husky, gentle and melancholy songs had reached into her darkness like strands of thin arteries feeding beads of life into the murkiness into which Luiza had been born.

Over the years the fado music they called saudade soon encapsulated her feelings, breathing and pulsating vitality through her soul and she began to sing with passion and nostalgia beyond her years, creating a longing and restlessness for something unknown. Something that encompassed her deepest emotions and her passions.

Luiza kissed her fingers, touched them to the waxy head of the Virgin Mary, said a quick prayer and crossed herself.

***

Luiza stood in the centre of the stage. Her straight shoulders illuminated only by the flickering of worn candle stubs and glowing cigarette-ends.

A simple black dress clung to her curvy figure and thick dark hair cascaded around her shoulders. Her closed eyes were framed by long black lashes making her seem vulnerable, and painfully beautiful.

Luiza sensed the atmosphere. She heard the hissing of a burning candle, a suppressed cough, a quiet murmur until there was stillness. And then, when all she heard was the gentle rise and beating of their hearts, in unison to the rhythm of her songs, she led them to places they had never before experienced.

She discovered an awareness and consciousness that engulfed her soul and lifted in her in a passion she had never known, and in return, she received from the audience their warmth and love, radiating from those who relished her voice and modulation of her tone.

She sang jazz, gospel, and soul music, but tonight, she was happiest singing fado. It was usually associated with poverty and sadness, and she often changed the beat and rhythmic tones so the songs became distinctive of her personality, and those who recognised music could not fail to appreciate her imaginative originality.

The faddista was expected to remain controlled and dignified. Like her idol, the famous Amalia Rodrigues, Luiza retained her motionless posture as her melancholic voice filled the room and the softly growing palpitation of emotion surged like an invisible electric current.

With her senses heightened, she felt the heat of the minuscule spotlight above her head, smelled wine from the breath of those seated at the front tables, and she tasted the words of her songs.

One by one the nostalgic folk music brought sadness to her heart, filling her lungs, draining her emotions as they seeped from her body. She lived it and she felt it. She sensed failure, hope and desolation. Until finally, at the end, as she took a last deep-lamented breath, silence reverberated around the room before spontaneous applause erupted.

Luiza bowed her head.

Very slowly, she descended the small platform

where she knew Cecilia would be waiting, but when she stumbled, it wasn't her sister's hand, but the fingers of a stranger that grasped her elbow.

"You remind me of Marisa dos Reis Nunes," the stranger said. "But you are more beautiful. You are more composed." His mouth was extraordinarily close and she tilted her head. His gentle words seemed to tickle the lobe of her ear which took her by surprise and her body shivered.

Beside her, Cecilia's voice was breathless. "Luiza is far superior. Marisa is popular and contemporary. Luiza's voice is richer and far more seductive."

Luiza frowned and Cecilia continued.

"Have you never heard her record or downloaded her music?" she spoke excitedly, and Luiza gasped at her sister's audacity and the enormity of her lies. "Alma was her best-selling album for 2008 in Brazil, and her second album História that she released last year, is one of the fastest selling folk albums of all times."

The stranger's voice was thoughtful and it held the trace of a smile. "Her voice has a seductive quality and she is very special. "My name is Otavio Seicheira," he added, "and I am pleased I had the opportunity to hear you sing."

The sound of his voice made tiny hairs on the back of Luiza's neck tingle. Had she been able to see him, she would have seen a man twenty years her senior with long hair, pockmarked-olive skin, gypsy green eyes and a wide mouth. Instead, Luiza smelled spicy cologne, a faint tinge of garlic, and lemon from his hair.

"I am in awe," he said softly. "Of your beautiful voice."

Luiza moved in the direction of the bar. She was unsettled. Who was this man? Besides, Luiza had never made an album in Brazil, or anywhere for that matter. How could her sister tell these lies?

"Who is that man, Christiano?" she asked, as the waiter guided her to a stool.

"Otavio Seicheira? He used to be a big music promoter. Is he here to see you?"

"No! No….Why would he?" She sipped the water that Christiano pressed into her hand and she shifted her position on the stool, away from the crowd, so that she could think in peace but Cecilia arrived a few minutes later to stand at her elbow.

"Listen, Luiza! Otavio has a proposal for us. Ask her Otavio."

"How would you feel if...?" Otavio paused, the question dangling in the darkness between them, and Luiza took a sharp intake of breath. "Would you be willing to sing with a full orchestra on stage? You see, on the Dia de Portugal, we are hosting one of the biggest concerts in Europe. I want to promote harmony across borders and between countries as a respect to all cultures and beliefs," he spoke quickly, his voice gaining momentum and enthusiasm as he explained. "I want to mix music and musicians from all over the world, combining styles and the richness of languages; using contrasts of sounds and rhythms to unite us all in harmony."

Was that warm cognac on his breath?

"And I want you to perform in Lisbon with a backdrop of the beautiful pastel-coloured houses and the majestic Tagus River under a beautiful full moon..." he paused. "I believe you would be stunning."

"What date?" asked Cecilia. "When?"

But it was Luiza who responded. "The Dia de Camões is named after Luís Vaz de Camõs the 16th century poet and adventurer. It's in six weeks' time Cecilia, on the tenth of June."

"Perfect," Cecilia said. "We are free."

"I cannot go," Luiza said quietly. She sensed the warmth of the stranger's stare on her closed eye lids before she continued speaking. "Cecilia was joking when she said I had made recordings in Brazil. I haven't. I am not famous. I'm - I'm just an ordinary faddisa trained by my mother."

Otavio laughed. "Believe me Luiza, when I say there is nothing ordinary about you. And, as for your imaginative sister, well perhaps she has a vision of your future. You will make an album. I will arrange it. The world must hear your voice."

Luiza bit her lip. She felt a surge of anticipation but how could she sing with a big orchestra? What would her mother say? And, she was sure Papa would not let her go to Lisbon with a stranger.

Otavio regarded the beautiful young woman. He was desperate to revive his flagging career and it had been his idea to orchestrate the biggest concert ever performed in Lisbon. A detour to the Algarve had been an irritant, but now he realised, it was just what he needed. She would be his hidden gemstone.

In his pocket, he clutched a badly written and crumpled letter, in Cecilia's childish handwriting, begging him to hear her sister sing.

What an opportunity this would be to promote this soulfully innovative and blind faddista to the world.

She was his destiny.

That's Not Funny

Mini Chapman kicks her legs. She stretches out cupped hands slicing the water. Her head tilts to one side as she breathes rhythmically through her mouth. She imagines she is swimming the Atlantic, being chased by sharks, tossed by giant stormy waves, and will arrive to victorious crowds holding banners and chanting her name.

John will be there - waiting.

He will help her from the water, kiss her cheek, and they will pose for photographs, smiling and laughing, celebrating her victory.

She leaves the pool dripping water, removes her goggles, slides her feet into flip-flops, and wraps a towel around her waist. She is seventy-four years old and four feet nine inches tall, and after swimming ten lengths of the pool she feels euphoric as if she has crossed the Atlantic.

But there is no-one waiting for her.

There's time for a quick shower before the kids come out of school.

She washes chlorine from her body, rinses her hair and towels herself dry before going into the changing room which is divided into three separate sections. In each section - on the left are lockers, in the middle is a wooden bench, and along the wall on the right - there are long, waist-high mirrors.

At right angles, like a T-bar, there is another mirror and a counter with hairdryers, boxes of tissues and creams.

Mini doesn't pause to look at her reflection. She sits on the bench and presses her nose to her arm, inhaling the scent of the lavender shower gel, and very slowly she begins to add moisturiser to her skin.

She reaches into the locker and is sliding her gym bag across the floor when she hears a voice in the far section of the changing area.

"I'm going to have to do it Rose. I have thought about it long and hard but it's the only solution…"

Mini thought she was alone.

"I have to kill him." The woman's voice is deep and she sighs heavily.

She pauses, her bare back is bent over her gym bag.

"I've thought about shooting him, you know, pretending it was a break-in or something like that. I could say that he went downstairs and surprised intruders but where would I get a gun, Rose?"

Mini waits, her bag is only half way to her feet.

"Off the internet?" Rose's voice is pitched higher. She sounds nervous and unsure. "I think you can buy most things on it."

"Umm, but the police could probably trace that. That's the first thing they would do, isn't it? Maybe I could stab him."

Rose's voice is muffled as if she's slipping her jumper over her head. "That's quite violent, and besides, think of all that blood."

"Did you say blood?"

Rose pulls herself free and her voice is clear. "Yes, you'd be covered in the stuff."

"Oh right! I suppose I would..." The woman with

the deep voice seems to consider before speaking again. "Well, how about poison?"

"That's neater and far cleaner," agrees Rose. "Wasn't there a case recently with a Russian spy who was stabbed with an umbrella dipped in poison? Could you get hold of some of that?"

Mini begins trembling. Very slowly she pulls underwear from her bag. She crouches on the floor and she slides her bra around her waist and over her small breasts, her fingers fumbling with the hooks.

"Maybe I could just run him over."

"And damage your Mercedes, Fiona?"

"Oh, come on Rose! I have to kill him somehow. I don't care about the car! He abuses me and beats me at every opportunity. He's raped me countless times and humiliates me at every opportunity. He's pure evil. I have to kill him. Help me," Fiona pleads. "Come up with some ideas."

Mini Chapman's knees are sore from the tiles on the floor. She has cramp in her left foot and a pain begins thumping in her chest. She hardly dares to breathe. Her pants are twisted and she kicks her foot to shake them loose, struggling to pull them over her ankles as quietly as possible.

"Couldn't you hire someone to kill him? I mean, you must have contacts in the wine business," Rose says.

"I think that happened to a woman before? I read it in the papers. She ran a pub or something and she hired an assassin to murder her husband, but the killer got caught and spilled the beans?"

Mini smothers a gasp. Her arm catches in her blouse, she hears a small rip and sees a tear the size of a bullet wound.

"No!" Fiona whispers. "It has to be a secret. If I hire someone, I'd have to kill them afterwards."

The buttons on the blouse seem too big and Mini fumbles.

"In fact, I'd have to kill anyone who even knew I was contemplating killing him. That's what happens. One murder always leads to another. I'm not a violent woman but..."

Mini discards her half open blouse and grabs her trousers.

"I must do it myself." Fiona's voice sounds resolute. "It has to be the perfect murder but I'll need an alibi."

"What about an act of frenzy? Self-defence or something, after all, he's been particularly brutal, couldn't you kill him then?"

"I don't want Robert to wake up–"

"Robert..." said Rose.

"Yes, he's only five. It would damage him for life."

"Oh, yes, that's true."

There is silence.

Mini Chapman holds her breath. She is frightened to make a noise. Her heart begins tugging at her throat then Rose speaks again.

"Could you make it look like suicide?"

Mini exhales. She pulls a jumper from the bag and, in doing so, her house keys rattle free and clatter to the floor. Mini freezes.

"I suppose I could somehow tie him up and put a noose around his neck."

Mini's throat constricts. She pushes her damp

head through her jumper and winds a chequered scarf around her neck.

"I suppose, I could say he was depressed, that might work," Fiona continues.

Still crouching on the floor, Mini leans around the corner of the lockers and steals a quick glimpse of the women through the mirror. She ducks back down when the blond one, Fiona, with thin lips and piggy eyes, looks up.

She looks like a killer.

The redhead - Rose - has green-eyes that glint like granite. She looks evil.

"Um…' Rose says. "Wouldn't his friends have to say to the police they noticed he was a little down? That wouldn't stand up to much questioning afterwards would it?"

"Oh, for heaven's sake, Rose, how hard can it be to murder your own husband?" There's a loud bang as Fiona slaps her shoes angrily on the bench.

Mini jumps.

She waits for her heart to settle then begins to pull her boots from the locker.

"This is ridiculous! People are doing it every day of the week. Pick up any newspaper. It's in there the whole time. It's so frustrating. This is really doing my head in. I just want to strangle the bastard."

Mini is sitting on the floor, her back against the bench, struggling with the laces.

"That's it! I'll strangle him. I'll get him drunk then I'll put my fingers around his neck and squeeze hard."

The scarf around Mini's neck begins to tighten.

"I'll cut off the air going into his body. If I

41

partially drug him, he wouldn't have the energy to fight back. He would writhe and squirm..."

Mini feels dizzy and suddenly very hot. Perspiration forms on her damp forehead and her breathing becomes more rapid.

"His eyesight would blur, and he wouldn't be able to focus, and his chest would feel like lead, like a giant iron fist grabbing his heart. He wouldn't be able to breathe. He would gasp and shudder, and his legs would twitch..."

Mini's hand is at her throat. She is sucking air greedily and feels a dead weight on her chest. She panics. She can't find her other boot so she grabs her towel and begins to stuff it into her bag.

It won't fit.

"And he would fall to the ground…" Fiona slams her fist against the locker. "Dead!"

Mini faints.

The sound of the sea washes through her brain. It's like a roaring tsunami: black, tumultuous, overpowering, and when she comes around it's like there is an electric light buzzing in her ears and behind her eyes.

She is lying on cold tiles but her face is hot. Where's John?

She sees a blond woman. Her face is blurred and her lips are mouthing something Mini can't hear or understand. She tries to sit up but the redhead is holding her down. She can feel their iron hands restraining her arms.

She screams.

"Don't move Mrs Chapman! You've cut your head but it doesn't look too bad. It's only a small graze." Paula, the receptionist, is kneeling at her shoulder. Her voice is calm and soothing.

Mini struggles. There are noises in her head.

"I thought she was dead," Rose says.

Mini wrenches her arm away.

"Stay with me. Don't leave me, Paula." Mini Chapman grabs the receptionist's hand, and looks down at her shoeless foot. "I need my other boot."

"Don't worry Mrs Chapman. We won't leave you on your own." Paula passes Mini a plastic cup and Mini sips the water gratefully. "Fiona's already offered to drive you home."

"No! I won't go! I want my boot." Mini Chapman shouts. She pushes the plastic cup away and water spills onto the floor.

"Have you got family we could call?" asks Rose.

"Doesn't your son live in England, Mrs Chapman?" Paula speaks loudly and slowly like someone in hospital talking to a sick patient.

Mini Chapman doesn't reply. She hasn't got to seventy-four years of age by being anybody's fool.

She'll get the bus home as she always does.

Fiona kneels down so her eyes are at the same level as Mini Chapman's. "You're frightened aren't you? You heard our conversation, didn't you?" Fiona's pink eyes bore into hers.

"No!' Mini shakes her head. "I didn't hear anything. I'm quite deaf."

Fiona smiles slowly. "Come on then. Do you live on your own? I'll take you home." She stands up and offers Mini her hand.

"I want my boot." She sees it dangling from Rose's hand.

She pushes her towel into her gym bag. She doesn't care that she has wet hair. She will do what she always does and wait for the bus at the bottom of the road. She will be home in time to go to work at three o'clock.

"You can't be left alone." Fiona insists. Her hands are big, strong and capable, and Mini imagines them around her husband's throat.

The redhead dangles the boot provocatively in Mini's face and Mini snatches it.

"Are you off to work?" Paula asks. "She's a lollipop lady at the junior school in the high street, aren't you Mrs Chapman?"

"A lollipop lady? You'd better be careful,' Fiona says. "You've a cut on your head. You wouldn't want anything to happen."

"Happen?" Mini repeats. She gazes hypnotically into Fiona's small eyes.

"Yes, it can be quite dangerous on that busy road. You need to have your wits about you. Some drivers have no respect for the speed limit or pedestrian crossings. And with that bump on your head..."

Mini imagines Fiona behind the wheel of her blue Mercedes. I'd have to kill anyone who even knew I was contemplating killing him.

"You wouldn't want to have an accident, would you?" Fiona doesn't blink.

"You'd better be careful," Rose says. "Some drivers can be very careless..."

"Accidents happen so easily," Fiona adds.

They know she's a lollipop lady. They might wait for her near the school. She can hear the squeal of brakes and feel the thud of her body on the bonnet, and she sees the lollipop stick being tossed into the air, and her hat lying lifeless on the road.

"I've got friends… I'm having a party. I've got people staying with me. Young people, children…adults. They're all coming to my house…and they're staying with me," Mini says.

"That's nice..." Fiona eyes don't leave Mini's face.

"I have! I've lots of friends. And they all have children. My house is very busy. They're waiting for me. My husband is there too. Yes, John's there. He always stands at the window waiting for me. John is…John is a policeman..."

"Is he?" Fiona raises her eyebrows.

"Yes. He's a policeman." Mini stands up. She picks up her gym bag and hooks it over her shoulder. "I must go. I can't be late for him. He worries. Yes, he worries about me all the time..."

Paula is holding Mini's arm.

"I'm fine!" Mini pulls away. "John hates me to be late. He'd call the police if I wasn't home on time. He knows them all. Even though he's retired he knows every policeman in the town."

Mini divides a path between Fiona, Rose and Paula with an outstretched arm, like a lance, and they part like the Dead Sea.

"Everyone is frightened of my John - John's a policeman. He'll be waiting for me. They're all waiting for me." Mini walks quickly from the changing room, conscious of the stares burning her back and trying to ignore the shiver of fear creeping through her body.

Rose, Fiona and Paula stand in silence, then Paula shakes her head.

"Poor Mini," she says. "Her husband died three years ago. He wasn't a policeman. I think he had a shop in the high street." She turns her attention to Fiona. "You were very kind to offer to drive her home. I haven't seen you in the gym for ages, have you been busy writing? Did you finish your sequel to Dead Women don't tell Tales? I can't wait to read it."

Well -Trained
A shaggy dog's story

Sally Poole was asleep when the doorbell rang. Her body jolted awake. She was disorientated and wondered where she was. She had been dreaming of Jack. Dreaming he was still alive. She half expected to see him trotting between the kitchen and the lounge. He had always been highly strung, always too-ing and fro-ing, in the house and outside in the garden, fetching tools out of the shed and putting them back again. His behaviour had been comical, especially since the size of their garden patio was as big as a dog kennel, but she still missed him. She missed him each day and each year that he had been gone, and she had been left a widow.

The doorbell chimed again.

She had always called him her little Scottish terrier because he had been stocky, bandy-legged with short grey hair and an intense nervousness about him. Had he been there now he would have been at the door, alert and filled with curiosity.

The sound of the afternoon quiz show echoed loudly in the room. The people on the screen were exceptionally colourful, the clapping more enthusiastic and the host smiling more than normal.

She looked at her watch, taking the dial between her thumb and forefinger, and squinted hard. The rings on her fingers glistened in the half light and she shook the gold bracelets so they rested farther up her wrist.

In the hallway the bell chimed persistently.

She struggled out of the armchair, her joints creaking, back sore and her head aching. She turned off the television and snapped on a lamp. The evenings were drawing in, it wasn't yet tea time.

In the hallway she checked her reflection. She patted her grey hair into place, straightened the yellow and blue Hermes scarf at her neck, and tugged the hem of her brown cardigan.

Smart enough. She would do.

There had been warnings recently; local television campaigns, leaflets through the post and the stern reminder from her neighbour Edna Stevens. Never answer the door to strangers. Never let anyone inside. Never tell them you live alone.

Remembering Jack's steadfast training, Sally Poole unlocked the door. She opened it cautiously with the chain still on, and peered anxiously into the darkness of the street.

Standing on her front step was a thick-set man with black eyes. He had curly dark hair and shaggiest beard she'd ever seen. He was a doppelgänger for a black Alsatian.

Although the light was fading, and her eyes weren't as good as they used to be, she saw a clipboard in his hand. It was a big hairy hand and it reminded her of a paw. It made him look clumsy and inept.

Unlike an Alsatian he didn't snarl. Instead he smiled with a row of white canine teeth, held out an official badge and spoke softly. His voice was a low growl and she leaned forward to hear him speak.

"Sorry love, the electricity's about to go off in the street." He pointed down the dimly-lit road. "I finish at five and I'll not be back 'til Monday. You could be without electricity for the weekend. I could come in and fix a new switch to your socket and it'll all be done in a few minutes." He shook his head. "It's up to you, love." He rubbed his arms and stamped his feet. He wore a red cotton scarf tied at his neck and it contrasted with the blackness of his beard.

"Is it everywhere? In the whole street?"

"Yes love. Cable replacement. Choice is yours." He shrugged but his eyes smiled. "I can fix it now or leave it."

Sally had always classed herself as an elegant poodle. At seventy-five she was squarely built, well-proportioned and well-dressed. Reaching her hand to the scarf at her neck she was comforted by the silk against her fingers and she smiled. She wasn't adverse to a handsome face even at her age.

"I suppose the food in the freezer would melt?" she said, thinking aloud.

The doppelgänger revealed a row of large white teeth. His eyes were docile and pleading. "I'll leave it if you prefer, the choice is yours."

She leaned out of the door and looked down the street. It was a nice neighbourhood set in a quiet part of the town, her house set back from the road with a private garden. Darkness had descended quickly. Yellow street lamps were creating a misty and mysterious glow and it was foggier than she thought. Across the road a white van was parked, but elsewhere it was silent and deserted.

A biting cold November wind blew in around her legs, tugging and shaking her skirt at her knees. She was conscious of Jack's constant admonishment that all the heat would be escaping - and did she intend heating the whole street - so she smoothed her skirt against her legs, patted her hair and straightened the scarf. She wished she'd had time to put on some lipstick, and against all Jack's good advice, she unhooked the chain and let the stranger inside.

He looked relieved to be out of the cold and he stood on the mat shaking as if his eyes needed to adjust to the light, and his body shuddered as if adjusting to the warmth. He smiled gratefully and wiped his boots.

He is well-trained, Sally Poole thought appreciatively. "It's a filthy day," she said, pleased to have company.

"It is," he growled in agreement. "Where's the junction box? Under the stairs?"

He reminded her of Billie. Her son was a big soft-hearted boxer with a square face and strong legs. He didn't visit her often but when he did, she found him so handsome she just wanted to stare at his velvety face and big brown trusting eyes.

"Yes!" Sally pointed to the cupboard.

She wondered if she should offer him a cup of tea. Instead she asked, "Is there a problem in the whole street?"

But he didn't reply. He didn't hear her. He was already rummaging, a flashlight in his hands, between the coats.

Sally turned her back and walked along the

hallway, her footsteps sounding hollow on the parquet floor. She switched on a small lamp. "I think I'll call my friend Edna who lives next door," she added aloud. "She will know what's going on."

She was trying to remember Edna's telephone number when she heard a sound behind her. She half-turned as the Alsatian moved with lightning speed and in one bounding leap, he was behind her growling. It was a low, rumbling, primeval sound that reverberated throughout his body. His chest was shaking and his big paw grabbed her by the throat. He lifted her off her feet and slammed her to the wall. The back of her skull cracked and her head banged against his fist.

"Stay quiet bitch," he barked, saliva drooled from his mouth. His spittle landed on her cheeks. His breath was rancid. His eyes fiery red.

She was trapped under the weight of his body. Her hands dangled uselessly at her side, and her thoughts collided like a cosmic explosion; burglar, money, jewellery…rape?

She had to concentrate. She had to fight back. She was suffocating. She reached up and grabbed his jacket, his red neckerchief was blazing bright red like silk blood. She pushed against his chest but his grip tightened harder than cement, more solid than gold. The harder she fought, the more aroused he became, he pushed his lips against hers, panting and biting her mouth. Then he pulled the silk scarf at her neck tugging it tighter, strangling her senses and all her reason.

"You like it rough?" he hissed.

She couldn't believe this was happening.

Seconds seemed like minutes. It was as if it was happening to someone else and she was a bystander and would not be affected. There was a cobweb beside the crystal lampshade. It dangled in the air, decorated with a multitude of hues: blues, violets, purples and pinks. It was magnificent then it faded, losing its vibrancy and turned grey, then greyer then black.

His fingers gripped and tugged her skirt. He shoved it roughly above her waist and she felt his hardness and her own naked vulnerability.

She wanted to scream but instead Jack's training kicked in and with one final effort she reached out her right hand and thumped her fist, hard, on the lounge door.

The Alsatian barked at her, baring fanged teeth, saliva drooling down his chin, leaving wet damp patches on his red scarf. He fumbled roughly at his belt yelping with excitement.

Sally heard, before she saw, the pounding of paws, and an avalanche of legs, chasing and crashing down the stairs.

Barking. Shouting. Barking. Squealing. Barking. Howling. Barking.

Then she felt a release of pressure from her throat.

His hands flailed in the air. His eyes turned from animalistic pleasure to disbelief as he was dragged roughly from her and onto the floor. The Alsatian began sobbing, whimpering like a baby puppy as his legs thrashed and his body writhed and contorted in pain. He tried to use his arms to protect his face but it was a useless action.

Kurt and Fritz were merciless. Their bloody broad noses snorted as they tore at their prey, their black lips stained red, eyes closed and forehead wrinkled in concentration. Bite by bite they tore his clothes. His hair and his face. Then eventually he stopped whimpering. He didn't scream. He didn't cry out. Only the hammering of his arms against the floor broke their greedy attack. They continued their bloody meal, gnawing, tearing and swallowing. They licked, sucked and chewed; lying on their haunches, indulging in their kill. He lay motionless, curled up like a foetus, hunched against the wall as they ate him, morsel by morsel until the dead carcass was gone.

Sally leaned weakly against the wall rubbing her bruised neck. She gazed at the ceiling hardly daring to look at the gruesome scene on the floor. Her heart was pumping, her mouth, dry and sore. She coughed and wiped his taste from her lips and spat onto the floor.

In the kitchen she took a bucket from under the sink and poured in a large quantity of bleach and hot water. It was fortunate she didn't have a carpet in the hallway. That would be such a mess to roll up and very difficult to dispose of without getting caught. Carrying the bucket Sally walked cautiously. She squeezed the mop and began to wipe the floor. She mustn't be too hard on herself. It hadn't been her fault.

Kurt and Fritz lay looking at her.

"Oh, you were hungry boys," she said.

The dogs licked their lips. They wrinkled their nose at the disinfectant and Fritz sneezed. She banged the wall twice and they sat obediently like two marble fireside statues at the foot of the stairs. Their brown and black coats now splashed and tainted red, their heads raised high and proud.

"You'll need a bath," she said.

She finished mopping the hallway removing all traces of blood and bone, humming as she worked. She imagined Jack, too-ing and fro-ing, his inquisitive little legs taking him from the hallway to the kitchen and back, carrying fresh buckets of hot soapy water. She really felt quite lonely without her little Scottish terrier.

Afterwards, she wiped the vibrant cobweb from the wall, and brushed her hand on her skirt. She squeezed the mop into the bucket. All that remained of the doppelgänger was a small remnant of his red cotton scarf. She held it to the light and twisted it in her fingers. Perhaps she would keep it as a souvenir. A reminder of her victory. A trophy that she could wash and iron and wear like a medal for bravery. Her fight against adversity.

Jack had been right all along. It's just a matter of time. They'll get you in the end, he had said, and he was right.

Just like the burglar who shot him in a robbery two weeks before his sixtieth birthday. A month before he retired. Shot dead. Two days after the funeral Jack's partner in the police force had brought Kurt and Fritz to her house. There was a note and instructions from her dead husband. He knew all about training and self-defence. He had been training the dogs in secret.

One knock was to call the Rottweilers

Two knocks to sit as still as statues.

She had experimented with them both.

The third knock was the killer.

Sally Poole checked her reflection in the hall mirror, smoothed her clothes, patted her hair and retied her Hermes scarf.

All her friends and neighbours had said they were frightened. There had been a spate of illegal acts in the area, muggings, robberies and rapes, and the police could do nothing. Crimes went unreported and unsolved. No-one had time. Too much paperwork. Too few police. Too many drugs. Too many criminals. No time or resources. You couldn't rely on the Government or law and order. He would probably have been on parole in three months, and ready to attack someone else, Sally reasoned. She couldn't take that risk. What if it happened to someone who couldn't defend themselves like her neighbour and best friend Edna who was eighty-nine?

It was one honest citizen's stance against crime.

One woman's defence.

Kurt and Fritz sat motionless and silent at the bottom of the stairs.

They were well-trained.

The Chicken-Man's Grandson

It was the first time Miguel had taken the public bus back from the Sierra Nevada and it rocked slowly along Granada's busy street: stop, start, stop, start. He sat slumped in his seat, watching queues of tourists taking photographs of an old church, impatient locals pushing crossly past them, and groups of giggling young girls using the zebra crossing. The bus lurched forward again and then stopped.

A familiar face suddenly caught his eye. He sat up, leaned across his friend Igor and banged on the window where his reflection had been.

"Mama?" he shouted.

Igor stirred lethargically and he pushed Miguel's arm irritably from his chest.

"Mama?" Miguel whispered. "What's she doing here?" His breath steamed the window.

She was laughing. Her head was thrown back revealing a long throat and white even teeth against olive skin. Her eyes were shining happily.

"Who's the man?" Igor said, removing the ear piece of his IPod. They both turned in their seats. "He looks like a lawyer."

The man was distinguished with greying hair at his temples. He wore a stylish dark suit but what was more disconcerting, was that he had his arm around his mother's waist. She looked so vibrant and alive, it was a picture Miguel knew he would remember for the rest of his life.

He had never seen her looking so radiant and happy.

The bus jolted forward, Miguel lost his balance, and he banged in frustration on the window.

He had just experienced the most perfect week. The ski group left yesterday afternoon but his best friend Igor had bullied him to stay on the slopes. Miguel hadn't needed much persuasion. Snowboarding was his passion in winter as kite-surfing was his hobby in summer. Besides, it had taken his mind off everything else that had been going on at home. For a few days at least, dread and fear had receded to some inner place and he had forgotten about family problems, cutting curves on his snowboard down steep runs, weaving, dodging, jumping in deep powder snow and bright sunshine.

Now his muscles ached and his body was tired. His young face was tanned and two wide panda eyes stared back at his reflection in the window.

"They're both at it," he said flatly.

Igor fiddled with his IPod earphone. "Maybe it's nothing," he said, in a bored tone that suggested he'd seen it all before.

Miguel flopped back in his seat. "She's having an affair. They're going to split up - I just know it!"

"How old is she?" Igor's face looked elongated and was far too big for his short body. Even though he stood a head taller than Miguel it was as if his body hadn't grown in proportion.

Miguel shrugged.

"Well, how old is your sister that lives in

London?" Igor insisted.

"Ines is twenty-two and Carlos is twenty."

"Then you came along four years later."

Miguel nodded.

"Well, she must be in her forties then. They don't do it then. Women? Do they? That's why men have affairs. That's why Dad went off with Rosario last year. He told me that Mum never liked sex. Now Mum complains she can't get a boyfriend and she's at least five years younger than your Mama," Igor said.

Miguel pictured Igor's mother. She was worn, ugly and unkempt, but he said nothing.

"Are you going to say anything to them?" Igor said.

Miguel thumped the empty seat in front of him. "It was bad enough seeing Papa last week with Ingrid," he replied.

The image of his father with his girlfriend still burned in his mind. He had spent the afternoon in Marbella where Igor lived with his mother and they had gone to the souvenir shop where she worked. While Igor asked his mother for money Miguel had fingered the familiar cheap goods, castanets, shawls, fans, flamenco dresses, bullfighter hats and tacky ashtrays. That was when he caught sight of his father across the road in a very expensive restaurant.

"I thought your father's Swedish secretary was going out with that doctor from the hospital," Igor said.

"So did I. But Ingrid was flirting, and he was holding her hand. She was wearing his ring for God's sake!"

Miguel remembered how he had stood staring

until Igor had pulled him away saying, "It's what men do. We'll do it too." He had dragged Miguel down toward the beach where they sat on a low wall looking out to sea, not speaking, but that was last week, and now Igor wiped their breath from the bus window with his sleeve as he spoke.

"It's probably just casual sex. Dad tells me that it's better most of the time than with your partner. He's very happy with Rosario."

Miguel who had never talked about sex with his Papa looked at Igor. "Are you not embarrassed to talk like that with your father?"

"No. We're open and natural about it."

Miguel stared at his best friend. "The only thing Papa ever said to me is that, 'your family is the most precious thing you can ever have. I was only a chicken-man's son and they forbid your mother to marry me but we knew we loved each other. You, Carlos and Ines are more important to us than anything'" Miguel's eyes pricked with tears as he continued speaking his father's words. "'I may only be a chicken-man's son but I'll always look after my family.' He repeated it so often Igor, that it's the family joke, but who's laughing now?"

If only grandpa were still alive, Miguel thought, and he squeezed his eyes shut and clamped his jaw tightly together.

Miguel's favourite grandpa, Luis Romero, had owned a rotisserie in Malaga. He had worked long hours, day after day, week after week, summer after summer, roasting hundreds and thousands and probably even millions of chickens; stuffing them with herbs and garlic, and dousing them in white wine before turning them carefully on the spit to get crispy skin and moist meat. Miguel imagined no job more boring but he had loved his grandfather more than anyone. They had spoken about everything, played football together, walked in the Montes of Malaga, travelled to Tarifa to watch the kite-surfing. He had taught him how to swim, how to play racket ball and how to ski.

He had been Miguel's best friend and confidant until his sudden heart attack last year. He missed him every day.

"If grandpa knew Mama and Papa were destroying our family, he would have something to say," he said, but Igor had stuffed his earphones back in place and was leaning against the window. He was fast asleep and snoring.

It was dark when Miguel arrived home. He stored the snowboard in the garage and climbed the stairs of his home, a luxury villa, in the hills behind the illuminated city centre below.

Although he was tired, and his body tense, his mind was reeling. He opened the front door, dumped his bag in the hallway and unzipped his jacket.

His father called out a greeting, so Miguel wandered into the bright lights of the big kitchen blinking tired eyes. He shrugged off his ski jacket and slung it over a chair.

"Hola Miguel, I thought it was Mama who had come home." His father stood at the worktop, cutting salami, measuring each slice with his finger tip before chopping quickly and cleanly. His Papa glanced up. "You caught the sun." His eyes were wary and his smile forced.

Papa was smaller than Mama. He was thick set and sturdy, dark and clean cut. His expression was one of concentration as he wrapped the sausage and replaced it in the fridge. He took out a chunk of manchego and began chopping neat, small wedges. His shirt button was undone and his tie loose. "Was the snow good?" He uncorked a bottle of red wine and poured a large glass. "Bring the tapas. We'll go in the living room and wait for Mama."

It was more of a command than a request and Miguel felt his face flushing as he followed his father along the corridor. Had it been daylight and clear weather there would have been spectacular views from the floor-to-ceiling lounge windows, across the sea to the distant coastline of Morocco, now it was evening and dark. All Miguel saw was his shuffling reflection, his hunched shoulders and defeated body as he flopped onto the beige, leather sofa. He wondered if he should say something. If he should tell Papa that he saw his mother in the arms of another man laughing happily.

His father took a gulp of wine just as the front door opened. Miguel guessed it was Mama.

"Wait here," he commanded, and he jumped to his feet, almost spilling the glass as he shoved it quickly onto the coffee table.

In the reflection, Miguel saw his mother and father at the front door, their greeting was hurried and stilted and they disappeared into the kitchen.

Miguel waited, conscious of their hushed voices behind the closed door.

He knew what was coming and he had been told by Igor how to behave.

"Don't say anything. It will make everything worse. They'll be pathetic, apologetic, humble even, but shrug it off as if you're not bothered or you'll get caught up in all their emotion and guilt. Divorce is common now. You'll soon get used to it."

Miguel sighed. It all seemed so complicated. He just wanted to snowboard and kite-surf. Why did adults have to complicate it all? He picked up a piece of cheese and felt sick. He couldn't eat it. He put it back on the plate but his mother's voice echoed in his head. 'If you've touched it, you have to eat it', so he picked it up, and began nibbling slowly. Waiting for the inevitable.

It took them five minutes. He watched them in the reflection coming from the kitchen and down the corridor to where he sat, two shadows looming, casting a shroud of melancholy over his soul.

"Hola Miguel." His mother sat on the sofa beside him. Her face flushed.

His father sat on the other side of the coffee table, he picked up his glass and took a large gulp of wine, swallowed quickly and then took another.

Miguel studied his feet. He needed new trainers. He picked at the loose skin hanging around his thumb.

"Mama and I have something important to tell you…" his father began.

"I know! I know! Stop!" Miguel held his hands over his ears. "Stop! Just tell me one thing, have you told Carlos and Ines yet?"

"No, we wanted to tell you first," his mother sounded weary. She looked tired. Had she been crying?

"Ines will be upset," Miguel's voice sounded unusually loud.

"No, she won't," his father said gently, he reached over and placed his hand on Miguel's knee. "It will affect you the most. You are the only one living at home now…"

"Maybe it would be better, for all of us, if I told her. Then she won't worry about me and how I'm taking it." He pulled his knee from his father's touch.

"If that's what you want." His mother reached out and touched his hand but he flinched and moved away.

"You know, it doesn't mean that we don't love you," she said.

"Will I still live here with you?" He hated the way his voice was hardly a whisper. The swirling in his chest jumbled his insides, raged in his stomach and sent waves of bile into his mouth. His thoughts were fluttering, chaotic, like random snowflakes in a storm.

"Of course," she said, "Why not?"

His father had a lump of cheese half way to his open mouth.

"But I'll spend time with you, Papa won't I? Will you move out?"

His father's arm stopped mid-air. He replaced the cheese on the plate and Miguel wondered if he should tell his Papa to eat the cheese, after all he had touched it, but Mama hadn't seemed to notice. She was staring at him with a bewildered frown.

"Why would I move out?" his father asked.

"Don't you want to be with Ingrid?"

"Ingrid?" They both said simultaneously.

Miguel thought of Igor, and remembered his advice, shrug it off as if you don't care. "Yes Ingrid! Aren't you seeing her now because Mama doesn't want sex anymore?"

"Cariño…" His mother held up her hand in protest but Miguel continued raising his voice, he couldn't stop, it was as if the barrier had broken and his words gushed out.

"I saw you with her in that restaurant last week. You were smoking a cigar and drinking brandy, and you were holding her hand and she wore a ring." Then he turned to his mother. "And I saw you today. I saw you from the bus in Granada with that lawyer and he had his arm around your waist and you were laughing and you looked so happy–"

"That was Jorge," his mother said. "He isn't a lawyer. He's a specialist. He's one of you father's old school friends."

"A divorce specialist! You are both at it. You always said that your family is the most precious thing. Even when you weren't supposed to get married, because you were the chicken-man's son, and you had no money and Mama's family didn't want you to get together…Grandpa would be horrified with you…"

"Divorce?" she said, "who is getting divorced?"

Miguel looked from one to the other.

"Jorge is a baby specialist, cariño," she said.

"Baby?"

"We've been worried because of my age but, today, Jorge confirmed everything's okay."

Miguel looked closely at his mother. She had a healthy glow to her tired eyes and they filled with happy excited tears. She had put on weight around her tummy, and she had been behaving oddly. He turned to look at his father.

"And Ingrid?"

"We were celebrating her engagement to the doctor but he was called to an emergency in the hospital. Now what do you think about the baby?"

Miguel looked at their reflection in the window. He saw his precious family unit, three soon to be four, and he thought how excited Ines and Carlos would be and he began to smile.

"We thought we might call the baby Luis or Luisa, after your favourite grandpa."

The Unfinished Currach

The pub was noisy with the sound of glasses, voices, banter and laughter, and amid all the chaos stood Seamus Mallin. He held a pint of Guinness in his fist, and stood, as if he always had. As if he belonged. As if frozen in time. A ghostly presence of his past.

So, the rumours were true, Seamus had come back for the da's funeral.

Colum O'Toolin studied the man who stood between groups of drinkers at the bar. Twenty years had taken its toll. His once chestnut hair was now prematurely grey and spiked. There were deep ingrained ridges at the side of his mouth and an old crooked scar ran under his left eye.

When Seamus addressed the group his voice ebbed and flowed melodically and hypnotically, lulling like the lapping waves on the rippling tide of the Killary River in the West of Ireland, right outside the pub's front door.

The black pint loosened Seamus's tongue. He spoke effortlessly telling stories of his travels, his life and his experiences with the talent of a true storyteller. He described the boats he worked on, people he met and countries he visited. He laughed when he told tales about the bars around the world; a dockers' bar in Marseille, a jazz bar in New Orleans, an Irish pub in Melbourne. He talked about fights with the locals, scrapes with his lovers' husbands, and when he spoke about the beautiful women in Thailand the local men bantered with him.

"I bet you dipped your oar in a few, Seamus," called bearded Mike. The fisherman's voice rough like a stormy sea.

Seamus smiled slowly. "The girls in Malaysia are shaped like a beautiful Currach. Their prows were sticking provocatively out at me, so I had to oblige them, it would have been rude not to."

Colum watched as Seamus drew the outline of a woman's breast in the air with his free hand.

The men laughed with encouragement and slapped the counter of the bar for another round, as Seamus continued, "Only out of politeness, mind, being the gentleman, I am."

"Bet you had to row yourself out of trouble more than once," Frankie said, his arms the size of a whale.

Seamus's eyes were the colour of the deep green Fjord on a blustery winter's day where Colum had fished each day since he left school. Colum had never travelled. He had never left Ireland. He blinked, picked up his pint and concentrated on the dark liquid. Memories of their school years formed in his mind. Images he had kept deliberately locked away now surfaced and bobbed like an unwelcome lifebuoy. They were too bright, too revealing and too illuminating.

***

The night after Colum's da's funeral there was a knock on the oak door.

"It's been a long time…" Seamus said, stepping

into the cottage. He gripped Colum's hand in a strong clasp then stood shaking rain from his coat and cap. "And Roisin, you're as beautiful as ever."

Colum's wife greeted Seamus with a mixture of awe and curiosity.

"Let's have your coat, Seamus," she said. "Sure, it's a rotten night out there. I wish I hadn't said I'd visit Mary. You remember my sister? But, besides it'll give you men a chance to catch up."

Roisin looked at her husband who sat in his customary chair beside the fire gazing at the hearth. She addressed Seamus but flicked her head toward Colum with a smile. "He seems to have disappeared inside himself."

She pushed Seamus toward a second chair, produced a bottle of Black Bush whiskey and took two glasses from the cupboard, aware that his eyes were travelling over her appreciatively.

"You don't look a day older Roisin than you were when we were all at school together. You're just as pretty and you still have those lovely ankles." Seamus winked.

"Leave it, Roisin. I'll pour. You can go now," Colum said suddenly, his dark eyes flashed. His mouth turned down.

"Ach, Seamus, away with you now and all your smooth talk," Roisin giggled, "It's been a long time since anyone paid me a compliment like that."

She placed a quick kiss on her husband's forehead, took her coat from the peg behind the door and slipped outside into the darkness; into the wind and the lashing rain.

The whiskey was rough on Colum's throat and

he welcomed the warmth that spread through his mouth and down to his lungs.

In the hearth, a log hissed then fell, causing embers to scatter violently sending a puff of smoke into the room. With the glass still in his hand Colum kicked the log back into place then bent over to add another.

"I thought we wouldn't speak again," Seamus's voice was soft. "I didn't think I'd ever come back."

"Don't pretend that would bother you."

"Twenty years is a long time."

"Twenty-one."

Seamus stood up. He picked up a framed photograph of Colum and Roisin taken on their wedding day and studied it for some minutes. Then he replaced it on the shelf and picked up another, one of a grinning teenage boy standing beside his father holding a big salmon caught in the river behind them. Then another, of their daughter laughing at her graduation. "You have good-looking children."

Colum had been watching him silently but as soon as Seamus spoke he turned his attention to his hands. They were capable and skilled with thick callused fingers and scars from accidents at sea. He turned his palms over and looked at the ingrained lines. Lines that he had once believed held the secrets to his future.

"Why are you back?" He didn't look up.

"I wanted to come home."

"What do you want?"

Seamus chewed his bottom lip before replying. "I want a boat-yard. I'm going to build Currachs…"

"No!" Colum's head shot up. His chin jutted out,

his eyes blazing and his hands shook.

Seamus stretched forward and gripped the neck of the whisky bottle, clinking the glasses roughly as he poured generous slugs for them both.

Wind hurled down the chimney, gasping and choking, and outside an unsecured gate banged.

"You can't," Colum insisted.

"I can. It's time. I've spent a lot of years doing what I don't want to do. Now it's time for what I want."

"It was your choice to go."

Rain lashed violently at the window pane.

"I'm back now."

"Things are different." Colum stood up and, on the far side of the room, he secured the rattling window, then pushed ragged blond hair from his face.

"I don't believe they are." Seamus stared hard at Colum. "Some things don't ever change."

Colum recognised Seamus was still the stronger of the two. Always the survivor, the warrior and the winner, but he wouldn't win this time. Not here in his town.

"No!" He tilted his head and drained the remains of his glass down his neck. He slapped it on the table with finality and walked to the door.

"It's time for you to go."

"The boys in the pub told me it's still there," Scamus said. He didn't move. "Mike and Frankie told me it's still in your barn… untouched."

Colum clenched his teeth together, his jaws working furiously to control his emotions and memories from the past.

Seamus took a pace forward and whispered, "It's

time." And with sudden energy and passion he grabbed his coat and pushed his arms into the warm fur.

"Come on! Let's go and look at it. Let's finish this once and for all."

He reached for the door handle but Colum sprang to life, slamming Seamus hard against the wall, his fingers clutched around his throat, steel eyes boring into the green depths of his old friend.

"No!"

Colum's spittle landed on Seamus's cheek just below the long deep scar that had barely missed his eye. It was a rough jagged scar, a violent tear in his weathered skin.

Seamus's body was hard. His chest muscles and the solidness of his shoulders were developed and formed from hours of hard manual labour at sea for over twenty years. He was the tougher of the two.

Very slowly and gently, Seamus unfurled Colum's fingers. "It'll be alright. Trust me."

Outside, under a half moon, loud waves cracked and broke over rocks. Wind howled across the open fields and, in the distance, a dog howled.

The old barn door creaked open.

Colum kicked a brick to wedge it firm, flicked a cord and a lone bulb dangled and swayed from a wooden beam. The cold air was musty and he waved his arm, chasing cobwebs from his cheeks and spiders from their rest.

Over the years the barn had become a dumping place for old furniture they no longer needed, old farming and fishing implements, rusted children's bicycles, tin barrows and bags of forgotten junk.

Colum began placing them all to one side until he saw the soiled yellow tarpaulin underneath and he paused.

But Seamus pushed him aside and began pulling the heavy plastic, tugging impatiently at the long ropes that bound the craft.

"Wait, Seamus!" Colum grabbed his friend's arm, conscious that it was the first time he had said that name aloud in over twenty years, and he savoured the name on his lips.

"I was always the impetuous one."

"Let's take the tarpaulin off together," Colum suggested.

They worked quietly and methodically like archaeologists on the verge of discovering something forgotten. The excitement building inside and between them, until the outline of the tarpaulin began to reveal the boat underneath.

Seamus held a corner of plastic aloft. "Ready?"

Slowly and carefully they lifted the plastic sheet. They rolled it to one side and stood under the glimmering light of the swinging bulb staring silently at the unfinished Currach.

Seamus whistled. It was a low sound of appreciation that Colum remembered from their youth and he smiled at the memory.

He ran his fingers along the spigot of carved wood which served as a rowlock. As children they had played in the barn and later as teenagers it was the natural and ideal place for them to build the traditional fishing boat. They had drawn plans for their first Currach, moulding wooden slats and covering it in canvas. Only the prow had a coating of black tar but the years had taken its toll and now the exposed frame was dry, cracked and split.

Colum cast his eyes around for the half-finished oars. Their work had been interrupted. Everything had remained unfinished.

Seamus stroked the outline of the wood, revelling in the distinctive shape of the Currach with its flat stern and curved prow. He caressed the skeleton of the upside down canoe held aloft by two trestles.

"Let's turn it over," he said, as if they were children again.

Standing one at each end they lifted it and placed it on the ground where the prow rose graciously up toward the beams of the dusty barn.

Seamus stood back and his green eyes filled with tears. "It wasn't easy, leaving…" He traced the outline of his scarred cheek with his thumb. "But I had no choice."

"You never said goodbye." The words Colum had spoken so often in his dreams, now sounded hollow, but the weight of them had been a heavy burden for years, in the empty cavern of his heart.

Seamus shook his head. "Your da knew."

"The da?"

"He saw us, over there." Seamus pointed to the corner of the barn where the boys had often lain together. "He cornered me that morning. He caught me against the wall of the pub and held a fish knife at my balls. He wanted to kill us both. I denied everything but he gouged me under the eye as a warning. He told me never to return. I was barely seventeen Colum. And I was frightened." Seamus coughed away a tear.

The wind gusted. The barn door rattled causing Colum to turn in alarm. A half memory, a hidden face at the crack in the door, a sense of someone watching or listening.

"I should have been braver but…" Seamus wiped his eye.

"The da was a bully. Now I know why he hated me so much." Colum leaned his hip against the Currach.

"I should have come back sooner." Seamus wiped his nose on his sleeve. "I should have stood up to him. If I was stronger. I could have…"

"It would never have worked. This is a small community, stuck in time, they would never have…"

"All the stories I told in the pub are lies, Colum. I covered up the truth. I'm sick of pretending. I can't go on like this anymore. It's all a sham."

Colum pushed his hair from his face. For years he had dreamed Seamus would come back, never believing he would.

"I thought of trying to find you but I wasn't brave enough either, Seamus. I couldn't leave here. I couldn't leave the Ma unprotected. I love Roisin and the kids but…" Colum kicked the dusty floor with his boot. "It's just not the same type of love."

Never had he felt the intensity and happiness that he felt when he was with Seamus. Worse still, was that in just a few hours, all the emotions and feelings he had pushed aside for twenty years were stirring again. Seamus had given him new hope, he had disturbed his dormant heart, and he felt the flickering of excitement. He wasn't willing to let it go again.

Colum traced his fingers lovingly along the prow of the Currach. "It'll be complicated but maybe we could have our boat-builder's yard after all."

In the glow of the swaying bare bulb Seamus's deep green eyes smiled. His left cheek was distorted, guarding the ragged scar that ran under his eye.

"Are we brave enough now?" he asked.

Conchita Cintron

"Her record stands as a rebuke to every man of us who has ever maintained that a woman must lose something of her femininity if she seeks to compete with men."
Orson Welles

Conchita Cintron mounted her white stallion with agility, wearing her usual grey high-waist jacket and stiff-brimmed Cordoban flat hat. She turned her horse around and cantered into the arena to the trumpeting sounds of the clarions.

We were in Spain and it was August 1949.

From behind the musty smelling barrier I watched Conchita, hoping she would become my future wife, my heart beating to the cheers and clapping of the crowd.

'Torrera,' 'Diosa Rubia,' Blonde Goddess, 'Diosa de Oro,' Golden Goddess, they shouted in excitement but, for some unknown reason, I felt a sense of foreboding.

I stood in the shade of the suffocating sun with other bullfighters, famous Spanish matadors; Manolo Vázquez and Antonio Ordóñez. A sirocco wind filled with fine grains of sand whirled like the angry and arrogant bull around us, as if looking for an exit from the ring.

Beside me stood my uncle, Ruy da Camara, once a renowned Portuguese rejoneador, a bullfighter on horseback, now trainer and mentor to Conchita. He watched her carefully in the ring, tapping a finger against his lips, deep in concentration. I could sense his heart beating, in time with mine, Conchita's, the bulls, and the horse's heart too. I felt we were locked in one rhythmic, hypnotic beat to the bull's pounding hooves and snorting breath that grew louder as the crowd fell silent with expectation.

Suddenly the bull charged recklessly, ramming his horns into a nearby shelter and a roar from the audience filled the arena.

The heat was suffocating.

I pulled at my collar. I had spent many years in South Africa and as a big-game hunter I could sense the bull's confusion and fear. I also recognised its lethal danger. When I was hunting I was in control but watching Conchita was unbearable for me.

A faint line of perspiration settled on my top lip. I could smell the sweat of the novillera beside me. His excitement palpable; he was itching to enter the ring. Then my attention returned to Conchita. She had been trained as a confident equestrian as well as a bullfighter; she held her back straight and her head high. Her bravado in the ring sparked a recent memory of an interview with a reporter from the New York Sun.

Her dark eyes had clouded over and she had tugged at the strap of her handbag as if they were the reins of her stallion. Her voice was low and thoughtful as she said that to show a qualm or a cringe before one thousand two hundred pounds of an enraged bull would be a sure death. Now, in the afternoon heat, I felt a shadow pass over me but looking up, the sky remained cloudless.

The crowd cheered, dragging me from my turmoil and I smile at her outward defiance and her façade of courage and determination. We had met only a few months ago and I was immediately attracted to the vulnerability in her heart, her sensitivity and her humble pride. I watched her horse dance, its tail held high, neatly side-stepping, almost taunting whilst zigzagging in front of the snorting beast.

At twenty-seven years of age Conchita had reached the pinnacle of the world's most dangerous sport. A sport dominated by men. Even now many matadors refused to attend the same corrida with her; it was beneath their pride but it only added to mine.

She had been raised in South America but she was a heroine here in Europe too. Recently she had won the admiration of the crowds throughout the Latin world, fighting in over four hundred events in Portugal, Spain and in several South American countries.

She had killed over seven hundred and fifty bulls. But to her frustration and anger, Franco's strict regime did not allow females to descend from a horse in the bullring because if the matador was gored, she may show flesh or nudity under her torn clothing, and that would offend their ideas of decency.

Conchita had laughed with scorn at the mere idea, but there was a jealous pang in my heart, I too would hate other men's eyes looking at her naked flesh.

Suddenly, her horse skidded on the blood soaked slippery sand. The crowd gasped. Ruy gripped the barrier. Conchita quickly regained her composure but not before I saw her dark eyes flicker in consternation. A small error could be deadly.

Ruy said to me recently that he thought Conchita would never marry and retire. But I was hoping she might do both for me. She was clever and independent. She didn't smoke, drink or wear make-up, and because of her slim figure and gentle demeanour she seemed to me as vulnerable as she was beautiful. I wanted to protect her.

In Spain, women have little independence, they still need the written permission of their husband to open a bank account. And although I loved this foreign land, it was a country still smarting from a civil war that had divided neighbours and families, where death had been commonplace and children of republican rebels were adopted and brainwashed by Franco's nationalistic followers.

I sighed heavily. I thought of the peace and quiet of my estate in Portugal and I imagined Conchita beside me cantering in the early mornings, riding across vast colourful fields of corn and maize, watching beautiful sun rises.

There were cries of, 'Óle!' and 'Bravo!' as Conchita wheeled her stallion around the ring demonstrating her art and her skill. She respected the bull; he was her adversary. It was not a blood-thirsty sport as many would think but more of a meeting of two brave spirits; bold and strong.

Conchita's face screwed up in concentration. I vaguely remembered Ruy telling me she had been injured once before in Mexico. A bull had gored her in the thigh but she had pushed doctors away and returned to the ring to kill the bull before fainting and falling unconscious. God forbid that were to happen again. I gripped the barrier, I couldn't shake the uneasy feeling that was spreading through my body.

Conchita had been trained from the age of eleven where she was raised in Peru. Ruy often recounted the story of his first meeting with Conchita in Lima.

He said, "There was a knock at the door and a tall, pretty child with dark blond hair and big round eyes of about eleven years old stood looking at me. She was dressed, as all children from the country, in overalls. 'What do you want?' I asked.

'A lesson,' she replied, thrusting me a crumpled note.

'Have you ridden a horse before?'

'I had a horse once. A friend of my parents gave it to me for my first Holy Communion.'

'And I knew then,' he would say, 'I saw the determination in her dark eyes. She would be famous."

Ruy often compared her with another strong and popular woman from Latin America, Eva Peron but for me there was no-one like Conchita.

The trumpets sounded for the kill to take place.

For years it had been Conchita's dream to fight on foot in Spain, even yesterday she had told a Spanish journalist she desired this more than anything, and it was as if the whole crowd knew it. They began calling out to her, encouraging her to fight on foot. My mouth felt suddenly dry, my head was shouting with the crowd but my heart willed her to stay in the saddle. She made a slight change of movement, twisted her torso and leaned forward. She had said to the journalist that the bull, to a certain extent, commits suicide when he charges. There's a little spot just forward of the shoulders which is not exposed to the matador's sword unless the bull is charging.

Her eyes narrowed and she gripped her reins. Her horse snorted as she tugged hard causing him to sidestep expertly from the charging bull. The crowd was delirious. Conchita wheeled her horse away and approached the presidential box.

The crowd hushed and with one body, and like me, they leaned forward straining to hear her ask permission to fight on foot.

It was denied.

The crowd shouted with disappointment and I sensed Conchita's fury and frustration by her rigid posture. Her horse trotted to the barrier and she avoided looking in my direction. She ripped off her spurs and dismounted. Her movements swift and ferocious. Avoiding the alguacil, the president's deputy, she grabbed a cape and sword and jumped into the ring. The crowd roared their appreciation and leapt to their feet.

Ruy laughed aloud and thumped me on the shoulder. "It'll probably be her last corrida," he shouted over the roar and applause.

Conchita stood on the hot bloody sand. Her sword poised high - waiting.

A dignified silence seemed to surround her aura, her concentration absolute. The bull dipped his head and charged. As it ran, I saw dark blood glistening, cascading from its thick neck. I held my breath. I could sense her thrill, her determination and her pride as she balanced onto the tip of her toes.

I straightened my back, a smile forming on my lips, I could sense her excitement. We would be a well matched couple.

As the fierce, snorting animal brushed passed her, she suddenly lowered her weapon, the crowd gasped, and she lightly grazed the spot with the tips of her fingers where she should have placed the sword.

The disorientated bull skidded, his breath laboured, his chest pounding as Conchita left the arena. The crowd was shouting in a frenzied uproar, waving white handkerchiefs, on their feet stamping their approval.

We hardly noticed the young novillera who took Conchita's place for the final kill. Instead, I watched helplessly as the uniformed guards gathered around Conchita and she was escorted away, and as she was arrested, the crowd began calling for her release.

Ruy clapped me on the back. "If she says yes, you'll have one hell of a marriage ahead of you, Francisco," he laughed.

With relief, I laughed too. But my sense of foreboding quickly returned. Franco's regime didn't take lightly the flouting of their strict rules. They had a way of punishing those who disobeyed, some people vanished permanently.

I tried to push through the throng of spectators, bullfighters and officials but my route was blocked. Whichever way I turned I was hemmed in, people pushed me with equal strength, a bald man with a moustache tried to duck under my arm, and a shorter man than me kicked out at my shins.

I saw Ruy's head disappear under the crowd just

as a younger man elbowed me in the cheek. I raised my fist to strike back but before I could bring it to down onto his head a roar ricocheted around the arena. My attention was distracted as Conchita appeared. The people around me stopped pushing and pulling and Ruy emerged disorientated but unscathed.

Together we watched in awe. Conchita looked magnificent. Triumphantly she strutted around the ring with deliberate steps, smiling and waving as she acknowledged the crowd's rapturous cries as they threw hats and wilting flowers into the ring, showering her with praise.

As a tribute to her courage and skill she was awarded the bull's ears and tail and she held the bloodied items proudly above her head. In an instant, across the crowd, her dark eyes met mine and I felt a wave of relief and I smiled back at her.

Conchita was pardoned almost immediately but those few minutes of anguish will remain forever etched clearly on my heart.

At this moment I believe I am the luckiest man in the world.

The Windfall

Bernadette's eyes glistened in the glow of the lamplight. She had seen suffering before and was accustomed to its darkness and its treachery. There was nothing anyone could do for Aunt Jean. It was almost over. Stifling a yawn, she stretched. Her head was in desperate need of fresh air and some signs of human activity. Her lungs were crying out for a cigarette.

Nurse McCallum's soft footsteps approached the bed and Bernadette felt the reassuring pressure of a hand on her shoulder, a small squeeze of solidarity, and accepted her compassionate smile.

She gathered her handbag from the floor and pulled on her coat. As she passed the nurse's station, two uniformed women whispered quietly and Bernadette imagined their conversation.

Isn't Bernadette dedicated? She's a saint. What a wonderful niece. Jean Longman is a lucky old lady.

Bernadette was too impatient to wait for the lift. She took the stairs downward, her tired feet echoing up the hollow stairwell to the floors above, where patients lay restless, sedated or anxious. Their worried families and friends had long since left for the night. Visiting hours were over.

At the hospital entrance Bernadette found a sheltered corner, pulled a cigarette from the packet, flicked her lighter and sucked hungrily on her cigarette. She glanced at her watch. It was almost midnight and A&E was busy.

Groups of people stood by the door chatting in concerned voices, smoking, rubbing brows and pacing in and out under the lamplight.

A middle-aged, grey haired man sitting in a wheel-chair had fallen asleep. His head had dropped forward to his chest at an awkward angle but the group didn't seem to notice or care, and from somewhere inside the building, a girl screamed.

Two uniformed paramedics appeared, doors slammed shut and the ambulance roared off into the night, its light flashing, leaving a blue glow in its wake.

Bernadette yawned.

It was her responsibility to stay here. She had to be there at the end, just like she had been with her mother, her uncle and her grandfather. It was her duty. She had never married, there were no children, just Ant and Dec, two miniature poodles waiting at home.

There was no rush. Besides, it was the least she could do.

She tapped her cigarette butt into the overflowing cylinder, spat a fluff of ash from her lip and debated lighting another but a gusty chill wind nipped at her neck so she pulled together the lapels of her moth-eaten coat, and went inside.

Back in the confines of the small side room she felt she was suffocating. Her nose was invaded by stale air, bleach and the remnants of dinner; cooked potatoes still floated in the air.

The recent fresh air was quickly sucked from the pores of her skin and the follicles of her hair. She could feel the oppressive and imminent threat of death and her lungs squeezed tight in anticipation of what lay ahead.

Aunt Jean was like a wizened dwarf with a walnut head peaking above the white sheet. She sensed Bernadette's return. She half-opened an eye, distorted by cataracts, and began to mumble.

Bernadette leaned forward. She couldn't decipher the disjointed names, breathless words and lost syllables.

Then all she saw were staring vacant eyes.

The old lady was dead.

Ten days later, John Caruthers leafed through the pages on his desk and regarded Bernadette over his rimless glasses.

He hadn't seen her since they were at school together some thirty years ago. He noticed there were still signs of her high cheek bones and her large brown eyes that had once flirted with him looked immeasurably sad. She was old-fashioned in her worn coat and sensible brogues. Her hair looked dishevelled and hung lifelessly around her shoulders. Life hadn't been kind to her and he felt a pang of unexpected sympathy.

By comparison, John had been far luckier. He had left school, studied law, met Marian and had four children. Now he sat poised in his deep leather chair in his expensive office, tanned from a recent golfing holiday on the south coast of Spain.

"You've always been so devoted to your family, Bernadette," John said. "Didn't you nurse your mother too?"

"Brian immigrated to Australia after he left

school and I was the only one left."

"I remember, you gave up your place at university."

Bernadette shook her head, unable to speak, and her eyes glazed over. She smiled a brave smile and hugged the tattered handbag on her lap.

An image of Mother Theresa sprang to his mind but then again, Bernadette was still a relatively young woman, and could be beautiful. She could make more of herself he thought.

"How are your family, John, I do hope they are well?" Bernadette interrupted his thoughts and raised her bowed head, and he saw her moist eyes. His heart ached. It was so kind of her to be concerned about the welfare of others.

He feigned heartiness. "Teenagers…boys! What can I say? One headache after another." He laughed.

Bernadette's half smile faded as if she had remembered a great loss. "You're lucky, John. There's nothing like family."

"Have you anyone left at all in England?"

She shook her head. "Just Uncle Jake, he's more of a second cousin really, living up north."

"Ah," John nodded and let his unspoken comment hang in the air. Then, as if conscious of the time, he passed the papers across the desk.

Bernadette signed her name with a small flourish on the documents that had been drawn up some months ago.

"I'm pleased your Aunt let me handle her affairs. I wish you would let me help you. If there's anything else I can do…" John deliberately left the sentence open, aware of the need for sensitivity. He could see

Bernadette was ready to leave his office and he offered his hand in farewell. She took it, almost as an afterthought, as if contemplating the loneliness stretching out in front of her.

After she had gone, John wondered how she would spend the nest-egg that had been left to her. He was pleased to note the Aunt had left her a tidy sum. If anyone deserved it, Bernadette did, more than anyone.

At home, Bernadette set her bag on the kitchen table, kicked off her tight sensible shoes and lit a cigarette. Ant and Dec ran around the kitchen barking at the back door which she opened, and they flew into the garden toward the dark hedges, falling over each other and chasing shadows.

Shrugging off her old coat, she tossed it into a small cupboard under the stairs and with a satisfying grunt she pulled the tight wig from her head.

Her reflection, in the kitchen window, revealed stylishly cropped black hair that emphasised her large eyes, well-sculptured cheek bones and generous mouth. A hot shower, some makeup, a layer of fake tan and she would look like a new woman. A glass of something chilled, she thought, and she would feel like a new woman.

John Caruthers was such a bore and filled with his own self-importance. If only he knew, she thought. She could buy and sell him outright. His pomposity had irritated her. But the way he had eyed her clothes and judged her image, as she wanted him to do, gave her a sense of satisfaction.

She pulled opened the fridge door and began mentally checking through the foil trays, noting the labels that the catering service had sent earlier that day; lobster thermidor; fillet mignon with duchess potatoes; and a generous apple pie. They had also left a selection of fine cheeses. Bernie smiled. Her stomach rumbled.

Her three dinner guests were her friends and business partners. Their new project, under discussion tonight, was taking over an ailing nursing home. It was in serious financial difficulties. Bernie had studied the finance proposal and had been to the site. It would be a cinch and very lucrative.

She just had to persuade her visitors.

All she had to do was take off these old clothes and put on one of her Chanel suits and Jimmy Choos and she would be the envy of her dinner guests.

They admired success.

But first she wanted to celebrate with a small glass of something chilled. The bottle of Moet popped and fizzled as she poured the liquid into a fluted glass. She leaned against the marble-topped counter contemplating her latest windfall.

It had been enriched by Aunt Jean's late husband, who had made a fortune in stocks and shares. It hadn't been a coincidence that in later years Bernie had befriended her Aunt and she remembered her grateful words.

"I'm so lucky," Aunt Jean had said on more than one occasion. "How would I have managed to sort out my papers? What would I have done?"

"Saint Bernadette," Bernie said aloud, and raised her glass in mock salute to her reflection. They had all called her that in the end; her grandfather, her mother, her uncle and now Aunt Jean.

Bernie wandered through her vast house with its large dining room and lounge that offered majestic views of the valley toward the sea.

She flicked a switch, and the garden was illuminated, revealing a trimmed lawn and tidy garden beds filled with winter pansies. Every penny of her inheritance had been hard earned. No-one deserved it more. It was business.

She checked her watch. There was probably time do a little more work before taking a shower and changing her clothes for her dinner party.

She picked up the telephone.

"Hi Uncle Jake? How are you today?"

Aunt Jean had been her mother's sister. Uncle Jake was her father's cousin. They lived at different ends of the country and had never spoken.

Bernie emphasised her vowels knowing he was half-deaf and had probably been waiting excitedly for her call. As she replied to Uncle Jake's feeble rasping, she noticed the glow of the mellow lamp-light outside and watched Ant and Dec chase each other, rolling over in the damp grass.

"I'll be over at the weekend to see you, Uncle Jake. It's just that my car has broken down and I haven't got the money to fix it, and with this rotten weather the bus service is so slow….I might not arrive until quite late."

Years of training and practice were paying off. She listened to him before replying.

"I couldn't possibly let you do that. It would cost you far too much." She sipped the bubbles and smiled, her voice became a purr.

"I know, and I want to see you too. It's just so

difficult with this job at the supermarket …and now they want to give me extra hours. They say it's because I'm single. I've no responsibilities at home and it's simply…awful. They think they can treat me badly just because I have no family."

Bernie paused and listened. She watched the dogs pawing the glass door waiting to be let inside.

"I know, I have you… and I really am so lucky. You are my family."

She admired her reflection, trailing a finger over the lip of the champagne bottle.

"I couldn't possibly accept that amount of money…..okay, well, if you insist…. We can talk about it at the weekend. Yes, of course I'll bring Ant and Dec. I know how much they mean to you." Bernie said goodbye and hung up.

It was always so much easier when she didn't have to live with them like she had her own mother.

It was also very convenient that Brian lived in Australia. It had been quite simple to persuade her grandfather that Brian didn't care. Bernie had also been cautious in passing on his long distance calls to their mother. It had been easy to pretend Brian hadn't been interested, or their mother was always out, and unable to take his calls. She had created a necessary distance between them and she knew that Brian was so hurt he wouldn't ever return to England.

After her mother died, the rift was too big. Brian didn't come home and everything was signed over to Bernie.

There was nothing wrong in that. They had been cared for, and it was up to them if they wanted to leave everything to her, in their Last Will and

Testament.

It was all about choices and sacrifices.

With a sigh, she opened the back door and watched Ant and Dec skip and yap around the kitchen, leaving a trail of dirty paw marks. They really were filthy animals but Uncle Jake loved them. They often sat on his knee while his old hands tickled, patted and stroked them. But it made her feel sick. Hopefully it wouldn't be for much longer. When he was gone, so would they. She was planning another cruise that would take her away for six months and she didn't intend to pay for yappy dogs in kennels.

There were a lot of lonely people with no family who went on cruises. They were only too ready to meet a good friend, someone to help them, someone to care for them. They might even be in need of a nursing home.

Smiling at her reflection, and thinking of her next windfall, Bernie raised her glass. Her eyes glistened in the glow of the lamplight. And failing that, Brian might also need her one day…

Plas Newydd

'But they still shall no more return to their house,
neither shall their place know them no more.'
JOB 7:10 - King James Bible

Mary couldn't believe she was eighty-five. Sometimes she felt eighteen. It was her body that betrayed her, and her face, like a wrinkled mask that stared forlornly from any reflected source. She didn't even know the stranger, the pretty impostor, in the photographs that adorned the grand-piano in the bay window of her Victorian home. But there she was, an attractive twenty-three year old smiling bride with Frank on her wedding day in Jerusalem just after the war. Beside that was one of Frank, with his treasured motorbike smiling into the sunshine, his eyes shining like brass buttons on his army uniform, and another one of them on a beach.

These were taken before they drove through Europe together, and before Orla.

She picked up her favourite photograph, taken a few years after that when Orla had been just a toddler whose excitement could not be contained. Her eyes had sparkled, there had been sand in her hair and wind on her cheeks. It had been one of those rare and special days on the beach in Britta's Bay without the usual chilly Irish breeze. One of those long summer evenings that Mary wanted to go on forever. It had left her skin tingling with its warmth and a pang in her heart as the sun set, for she knew the day would never be repeated.

Mary set the photograph back in its place and perched on the edge of her chintz sofa feeling a hint of warmth from the March sunshine through the window.

Her home seemed unusually quiet save for the slow ticking of her mother's clock on the mantelpiece that only emphasised the passing of her life.

Frank's death last year had left her feeling numb and alone. She followed the motions of life which were expected of her, shopping - weekly, eating - sparsely, sleeping - irregularly, but there was a continual and endless black hole in her life that made her feel empty and alone.

Orla had cajoled her like a child, 'onward and upward,' 'dust yourself down,' 'years ahead of you yet.'

But what, thought Mary, was the point? Especially with the bombshell Orla had dropped just a few weeks ago. They were leaving, moving abroad, emigrating.

Mary sighed, sat back and pulled the worn familiar cushions into her angular-shaped body. Thankfully, she had her home and her books which were her lifeline. They gave her access to hours of imaginary lives disconnected with her solitary existence. And today, as with most days, she picked up a book and drifted into another imaginary existence.

***

Sarah Ponsonby was born in 1755, she was the orphaned daughter of wealthy landowner in County Kilkenny. After the death of her remarried stepmother she lived with her father's cousin and went to a local boarding school. She had a troubled childhood but from the age of thirteen she knew exactly what she wanted....

***

Sally Parson wanted her father to leave her alone.

She wanted to be left in peace, in the privacy of her bedroom. She tried ignoring him by keeping her eyes firmly on a poster of Bright Star, her favourite film, stuck on the wall over his shoulder. She concentrated on Fanny Brice's unwavering and devoted love for the poet John Keats.

"You'll love it, Sally. Just imagine…" Alan's soft Dublin accent sounded dreamy, like it did when he teased Orla, her soon-to-be new step-mother. "Sun, sand, sea, and you can learn to surf too. "You'll easily make new friends…"

But Sally knew his enthusiasm had been fired up by Orla.

It was all her fault.

"I like it here. I don't want to go to a new place. I don't see why I can't stay behind with Emma. She used to look after me when you went on your work trips. She's my friend…"

"But Emma is much older than you, probably by fifteen years. Don't pick your nails, Sally."

He reached for her hand but Sally pulled away.

97

"Emma will want a husband and a family of her own one day…" He spoke but Sally didn't listen. He clearly didn't realise that neither she nor Emma wanted anyone else. They were happy together. And the thought of her half-packed bag under the bed made her feel giddy with excitement.

She was ready to escape. She would start a new life with Emma in a new place. Her mind was made up.

***

The canal path was Sally's favourite trail. They walked and ran and chased Frisky who, in turn and barking frantically, pursued the ducks. She stopped running and bent over, holding her knees gasping for air, but Emma continued running along the water's edge. She watched her gracefulness, she was like a gazelle, running effortlessly, her long stride pushing Frisky to go faster.

Sally gulped fresh air and tilted her chin toward the half-faced moon glistening back at her in the watery sunlight.

It was one of those special March days with clear skies and a chilly wind, and Sally felt the early stirrings of spring, spiralling through her senses. She squinted up at the moon and wondered what she would look like from there, looking back down at her. She would be smaller than the smallest dot on her school copy book, smaller even than that, with no apparent feelings, thoughts, ideas or emotions - too small to show up at all.

Imagine being that small and having no feelings?

The wind licked at her curls and she shoved them behind her ears. If every moment could be as free as this one, it would be heavenly. She didn't want the day to end.

In the distance, yellow daffodils bobbed brightly on the banks of the canal. The water looked murky and a few ducks sailed past, their noses high in the air. Frisky leaped up at Emma, trying to grab the stick from her hand, and Sally saw Emma's green eyes sparkle in excited delight.

Emma waited for Sally to catch her up. She had been reticent and quiet since returning from a conference in London a few days ago and Sally was waiting to see if the fresh air would help lighten her mood.

"Do you know that boy?" Emma nodded toward a curly-haired teenager in his school uniform farther up the path.

Sally recognised him from the class above hers, but she shrugged and looked across the canal in the opposite direction.

"He's got a lovely Labrador. And he's good looking! Come on, Sally! Let's go and talk to him."

But Sally turned away. She didn't want to speak to any boys. Why did Emma always try to get her to mix with other people? Her mood darkened. There was so much happening recently, moving abroad and now Emma's strange mood. Sally hadn't seen her for five long days and since she returned she had hardly spoken. It was as if she had something on her mind, something troubling her but when Sally asked, Emma had only said the conference had been boring but thankfully a few guys from Cork had made it fun, and had been a good craic.

Sally liked it best when Emma was teasing and happy, then she would quote some poetry, something romantic or funny. She bent down and pretended to tie her lace, she waited until the boy and the dog passed and she didn't look up.

"Was it a vision, or a waking dream?" Emma said dramatically and nudged her to her feet. "Do I wake or sleep?"

Sally giggled.

She felt a weight lift in her soul and her mood lightened. She loved it when Emma recited poetry. It was like she spoke to her heart making her feel warm, happy and secure. She reached out a hand but saw a flicker of consternation pass across Emma's face.

***

Sarah Ponsonby's lover was sixteen years her elder. But the biggest scandal at the time was that her lover's name was Lady Eleanor Butler. The first time they tried to elope, Sarah leapt out of a window, dressed as a man, armed with a pistol and her dog. A little later they were caught and forced to return. They had to wait several more years until they finally escaped together and took up residence in Wales where they became known as the Ladies of Llangollen. They found a small cottage which they renovated and renamed Plas Newydd - New Place - signifying their new life together.

***

Mary placed her book to one side and watched as Orla navigated her way through the lounge, balancing a tray with china cups and a selection of chocolate biscuits.

She pushed her crossword and Sudoku puzzles from the coffee table and concentrated as Orla poured milk, then tea, wondering if she would miss the normality of life at home when she moved abroad. What challenges would face her?

"Isn't Spain going through the recession too?" Mary asked, taking the teacup.

"Yes, but it is getting better there now," Orla replied.

"I remember going there with your father before Marbella was famous. They hadn't even built that port then…"

"Puerto Banus?"

"Yes, that's the one. It was only a field of olive trees." Mary bit into a biscuit. "We drove over the mountains from Granada to Malaga on the coast. I can still remember the sight of the sea as we came over the last hill shimmering like an apparition in the dessert. We were so excited. Then Frank's motorbike broke down and he hitched us a lift on the back of a pig truck." Mary smiled. "Black pigs they were with staring pink eyes. Frank said they were going to the market…"

Orla studied her mother silently. She hadn't touched her tea and she leaned forward clutching her palms together in earnest. "So, have you thought any more about moving?"

"No."

"Oh, for heaven sake, Mum!" Orla stood up and went to the window. "You can't stay here on you own."

"I don't want to go to a new place at my time of life. This is my home. Go to Spain Orla, but don't commit me to a horrible institution."

"It's called, sheltered housing."

Mary got up and walked slowly over to the window. They stood quietly together looking at the garden.

"The daffodils are early this year," Mary said.

"It'll be good for Sally." Orla's blue eyes held the same intensity as her mother's. "You know Sally's mother died in a road accident. She needs the stability of a family. So far she's spent more time with Emma, than with me or Alan. He travels so much…"

"Emma?"

"She's been a rock to Sally, ever since her mother – you know…died. But she's so much older than Sally… Sally's young, she should be with people of her own age having fun, on the beach…and…" Orla shrugged and turned away. "Oh, I don't know. I just want what's best - I don't want Sally getting hurt again. I want to protect her."

Mary looked at her daughter's earnest face. She would be a good mother.

"Alan does his best. He just doesn't notice these things."

Mary's long slim fingers reached for her daughter's hand. How often had she kissed these fingers? How could she have forgotten how soft Orla's hand felt in her own wrinkled palms?

"Life isn't simple, Orla. It doesn't always turn out how we want, happy or sad. It's always unpredictable."

In the garden, bright daffodils were bending and swinging in the breeze, it was one of Mary's favourite days, cloudless skies and a silver rising moon and it made her feel happy to be alive. Everything looked so pretty, so vibrant and full of life and colour.

"I wandered lonely as a cloud, That floats on high o'er vales and hills, When all at once I saw a crowd, A host, of golden daffodils…'"

"You always loved Wordsworth." Orla smiled.

"I would miss this garden." Mary thought then of the Ladies of Llangollen. They became renowned for their culture and for being refined and well read. They created a home together and received many visitors; Charles Darwin, Lady Caroline Lamb, Anna Seward, Madame de Genlis and Edmund Burke.

Mary remembered that William Wordsworth once dedicated a sonnet to them that ended;

'sisters in love, a love allowed to climb,
Even on this earth, above the reach of
Time.'

But she didn't mention this to Orla. It was neither the time nor the place.

***

Sally pulled the duvet tighter around her body and wedged the pillows behind her head. She could hear them downstairs still arguing, their voices floating up to her bedroom.

"I'm not saying we won't go to Spain, Alan.

What I'm saying is, is that maybe now isn't the right time. We may need to wait a while, you know until…"

"So? You're backing out now, Orla?"

"I'm not. It's just that I'm wondering if it really is for the best - for all of us. For Sally, her education, for us…. for my mother…"

"I thought we'd been through all this. And we decided …"

Sally's mobile phone rang. She grabbed it from the bedside table, still half-listening to the argument in the kitchen.

She saw Emma's name on her phone and she spoke without greeting.

"Guess what, Emma? I don't think we're going to Spain, now. They are downstairs fighting. I think Orla has changed her mind…"

Like her father, Sally was still digesting this change of mind, but she felt secretly pleased that Orla was on her side at last.

"Oh, Sally, that's brilliant. I'm so pleased for you."

Sally hesitated.

Her mind was made up. Her bag was still packed under the bed. She had been dreaming for endless nights of eloping with Emma and their new life together.

Would they still go, now that she wasn't moving to Spain?

"Sally? Guess what? I've got some good news too." Emma sounded serious. "You know that conference I went on and I told you there were some guys from Cork? Well, I met this guy Donal. He's so lovely and he's coming up to see me for the weekend. I can't wait for you to meet him."

Sally gazed at the poster on her wall. Bright Star.

"Sally? Are you there?"

"But what about me?"

"I'm your friend. I always will be. I'll always be here for you."

"But you didn't tell me."

"I wasn't sure Donal…"

"You didn't say anything before. I thought you…and I…I was ready to run away…"

"Sally, you have school to think of and…"

"To hell with school!" Sally shouted, and she let the phone fall from her hand where it gave a muffled thud onto the carpet.

She sat staring at the poster. Fanny Brice and John Keats, their heads bent together, eyes closed, about to kiss. "Would I were steadfast as thou art - ," she whispered and tears burned her eyes.

She could hear Emma's voice floating up from the floor. "Sally? Sally? Are you there?"

***

Eleanor Butler died in 1829 and her 'sweet love' Sarah Ponsonby passed away thirty months later. They were together for over thirty years and buried in the same grave in Llangollen, Wales.

***

Mary read quickly, her tired eyes flicking across the page. She finished the epilogue, closed the book and yawned. She turned it over in her hands to look at the image of the two women on the front cover. Then she lay down, curled on her side and closed her eyes.

She reached out a hand to stroke the sheet and she imagined Frank beside her. She thought of the shared headstone belonging to the two Ladies that rose far above other grave markers in Collen's graveyard, and the carefully carved words.

'But they still shall no more return to their house, neither shall their place know them no more.'

It was now engraved upon Mary's heart.

A Hot Day

Dawn threw her bag on the floor and slammed the car door. It clunked shut with finality like a coffin lid.

Billy Ocean blared out from the radio. When the Going Gets Tough, and the air conditioning was full blast. The other thing Dawn noticed was Mike's familiar aftershave. It was spicy and strong and it invaded her senses.

"Good day at school?" he asked. His fingers drummed the steering wheel to the beat of the song.

She ignored him, reached for the seat belt, tugged it over her shoulder and clicked it into place.

"There's Sally and Vanda." He nodded toward the pavement where two teenagers walked by, their heads bent together, as if sharing a secret.

They were clones of all the other girls exiting from the school; green skirts, white blouses and ties tugged at half-mast.

"They look much younger in uniform than they do at the weekend," he laughed.

Dawn tugged her skirt down.

"I could've walked home with them," she said.

"You know what your Mum's like. It's too dangerous."

"Yeah, let's all obey Mum!" Dawn shrugged, her eyes still on her friends.

"Do you want to offer them a lift?"

"No!"

She reached out and changed the radio station at

the same time Mike reached for the gear stick. Their arms brushed, their hairs tingled against the others' skin. He pulled away. Dawn put her hand in her lap.

Rap music blared out.

Mike turned down the volume and glanced at Dawn, but she continued to stare out of the window. Her green eyes were sulky and her rust-colour hair had come loose from its red ribbon. It was matted and she began picking at the split ends.

"Your hair needs a good brush. Did you have ballet today?" He swung the car into gear and pulled into the traffic.

A car hooted.

"Watch out! Concentrate on the road!"

"They didn't hoot at me."

"They did!"

The traffic was always busy, but today everyone wanted to get home and they were in a hurry. It was Thursday and it was hot, and the unexpected May heat-wave was due to last all weekend.

Dawn sank back into the leather seat and closed her eyes. She parted her legs and pointed her knees toward the vent of the air conditioning. She sighed and licked her lips.

"Thirsty?" Mike glanced at her, looked away and rubbed his chin.

Dawn heard the raspy sound of his shadowed cheeks and looked up at his profile. His nose was long and his lips too generous for a man. His cheeks were sunken and his long greying hair made him seem older than his forty-two years. Chest hair sprouted from the top of his green Lacoste T-shirt and there was an ink stain, shaped like the continent of

India, on his beige chinos.

"I made some chilled soda and lemon. I made it especially," he said.

Dawn turned her eyes away from the dark hairs at his wrist. His fingers were drumming rhythmically to the rap music.

She gazed outside at the houses as they crossed town, past housing estates, the 'rough' areas, past the semi-detached bungalows where she had lived with her mother. This was before they had moved in to Mike's home nine months ago, just after her sixteenth birthday. A month later he had produced a ring for her mother but they still hadn't mentioned marriage.

"I thought you had too much work to collect me."

"I am busy," he smiled. "But you know Thursdays are impossible for your Mum at the clinic."

"When are things never impossible for her?"

He turned to look at her but she glanced away.

"Any homework?"

Silence.

"Well?"

"Bit!"

"Anything I can help you with?"

"No."

"You liked the music from Don Giovanni I played the last time for your music exam."

"No."

"I thought you enjoyed that…play."

He turned the Mercedes off the road and the car sped into the driveway, spewing gravel into the air like hard confetti, coming to rest in front of the imposing red-bricked building.

Mike turned in his seat. He took the strand of hair that Dawn sucked and pushed it behind her ear. "I want to help," he said.

Inside the house, Dawn threw her schoolbag on the hall-floor. She followed Mike through to the kitchen and watched as he opened the fridge, took two glasses from the shelf and poured generous measures of soda and lemon for them both. He pulled out a large knife and cut wedges of lime on the chopping board.

"Let's go through to the conservatory. We can wait for your Mum there."

She followed him.

The windows and French doors were open but there was no air and it was hot and muggy. The radio was programmed to a classical channel and a soft voice spoke suggestively in the background.

Dawn kicked off her shoes and sat curled on the beige sofa. She tugged down the hem of her skirt as he handed her the glass. The cold ice clinked against the glass. She sipped, then opening her mouth she took a cube in its entirety, and sucked loudly.

Mike sat beside her and crossed his legs.

"Nice?"

She nodded.

He smiled then reached over and pressed his glass against her bare thigh.

When she gasped he laughed aloud.

She looked at him from under her long eye lashes. Wiping the spittle that had tumbled from her mouth with the back of her hand, she raised her glass and spat the remaining bit of ice back into the glass.

"Homework?" she said. "Before Mum gets here?"

He nodded, sighed and leaned back against the cushions. He closed his eyes. His legs were parted. His glass balanced on his thigh, tilted at a dangerous angle.

Dawn stood up and looked down at him for a few seconds. Then she walked to the hallway, fetched her schoolbag and returned to the dining room. She placed the bag on a chair and removed a paperback.

The table was full of his books, newspapers and laptop. There was an assortment of pens and pencils and reams of printed papers, two dirty mugs and a small plate with crumbs. It looked as if he had jumped up and left all his work to drive to school and collect her.

Dawn licked her finger, pressed it against the crumbs, then put her finger in her mouth.

She turned to look through to the conservatory.

Mike hadn't moved. His legs were spread open and he looked asleep. There were dark circles around his eyes.

"Macbeth!" She held up a worn copy. "Or are you too tired?"

"One of my favourites," he said.

He rubbed his eyes and stood up. He moved toward her, carrying his glass. The cubes rattled.

"Art thou not some fatal vision? Is this a dagger I see before me? The handle pointing toward my hand?" He held out his free hand pretending it held a weapon. He deepened his voice. "Come let me clutch thee…" He circled where she stood. "I have thee not, yet I see thee still…."

She giggled.

Her blouse was tight against her breasts. His breath was hot on her neck and there were raised goose bumps on her arm.

"Have you read it?" he murmured.

"No," her voice was barely a whisper.

"It's all about temptation." He blew a stream of breath on her neck. "You look hot, are you perspiring?"

He pressed his glass against her forehead. She closed her eyes pressing her head returning the pressure. The red ribbon from her hair fell to the floor.

Seconds later she opened her eyes. She reached out her chin and licked the side of his glass. He tilted it, and she slurped greedily, the lime wedge bumping at her lips, and when he pulled the glass quickly away, the liquid spilt down her chin and onto her blouse.

She laughed.

He wiped her blouse with his palm and her nipples pushed out against the fabric.

"Do you want to sit down?"

She nodded at the busy table. "Do you have time for me?"

"I have a deadline, but it can wait."

She sat down and opened the book.

"When shall we three meet again…," she read.

He stood behind her and began to caress the back of her neck.

"They are temptresses. Three evil witches," he interrupted, "they lure him, into doing something……very, very bad…"

Silence.

"Sex?" she asked.

"No, worse…." He leaned over her. "Murder!" The word, whispered on her ear, was carried on each individual, small, delicate hair follicle, rippling like an undulating wave across the sea.

She shivered.

"For love?"

"No…power and control."

She turned to look at him.

Their faces were close. Their lips almost touching.

He continued to rub his fingers in a circular motion, delving into the nape of her neck under her matted and ruffled hair.

He stood straight and her eyes were at the level of his belt.

"You know all about temptation," he whispered.

She closed her eyes, placed her lips against the bulge in his trousers and blew her hot breath against him.

He removed his fingers and when she opened her eyes he was no longer there.

She found him in the kitchen.

He had his back to her. He stood with a bottle of cold beer in his hand. He flipped the cap and looked at her.

"Well?" she said.

He sipped his beer and watched her.

"Your Mum will be home soon."

They both looked up at the ticking wall-clock.

"So?" She tugged loose her tie.

He watched.

She began to unbutton her blouse.

He shook his head. "No."

She nodded. Her eyes never left his face. She took a few steps closer to him. Her white bra, virginal and bright, against her pale freckled skin. She hoisted up her skirt revealing a red thong. She took his hand and pulled it toward her crotch.

His finger touched her dampness. She reached for his other hand pushing the cold bottle against her bush.

She murmured.

Outside there was the noise of an engine, the crunch of gravel and a quick skid of breaks. A car door slammed.

He pulled his fingers away.

The front door opened.

Dawn pulled down her skirt.

There were quick steps on the hallway tiles.

Dawn buttoned her blouse.

"I'm home!" A woman's voice called out.

Dawn turned away.

The carving knife was on the worktop. Its blade glistening in the sunlight like a tempting flashing diamond. She picked it up.

Her mother appeared in the doorway.

"Hi, you two," she said.

"Hi darling." Mike caught her in a big hug. He pressed the damp beer bottle against her cheek and she pushed him away laughing.

"Dawn? What are you doing with that knife?"

Silence.

"Put it down." She threw her handbag on the counter. "God, it's stifling in here. There's no air. I'm so hot." She grabbed Mike's beer bottle and took a long drink.

Afterwards she smiled. "I'm very, very, hot." Her eyes never left his face and she leaned toward him.

Dawn watched as their lips met.

Mike's hand clasped her mother's arse and began to massage her pert bum. She saw his tongue enter her mother's mouth. She felt it probing against her mother's teeth.

Dawn held the knife at an angle catching it in the sunlight and aimed the shining shadow onto Mike's face. As a child, she had called the reflected light a fairy, now it danced brightly on his closed eyelids.

Almost immediately he opened his eyes. His mouth and tongue still working her mother's lips. He stared at her.

Dawn smiled back.

Jasmine

Patricia O'Reilly stood at the supermarket window watching three men redecorating the building across the road, thinking about the film she had seen a few weeks ago, Slumdog Millionaire.

"The Indians are moving in, then," Ciara said, standing beside her.

She looked at her daughter's features, a younger version of her. Auburn coloured hair, and the same frown between worried dark green eyes.

"It will be good for the village," Patricia replied.

"This is rural Ireland." Ciara laughed. "We've four pubs, two churches, a bed and breakfast and a chippie in the village, so I can't see how there'll be a demand for an Indian restaurant too."

"It's called variety, Ciara. A bit of competition is always good for business." Patricia left the till and walked to the back of the shop. She still had stock to order.

"You wouldn't be wanting competition if it was a big supermarket chain opening up," Ciara shouted at her mother's retreating back.

Minutes later Patricia returned with the stock book and began checking the shelves at the front, methodically and precisely, just as she had been doing for the past thirty years.

Ciara continued to stand at the window. Her vision of Billy was blurred by heavy raindrops against the window as he locked the butcher's shop, hitched blue jeans over his skinny hips and ran across the square into Murphy's pub.

"Maybe you'd better show a little more interest in Billy," Patricia said looking at Ciara's gloomy face. "Jessica seems very keen on him."

Until a year ago, Jessica had been a spotty teenager with braces, now she was transformed into a WAG look-a-like and the local favourite barmaid.

"That hussy," Ciara muttered, and her skin began tingling with a premonition that everything was beginning to go wrong in her life.

"I don't know what you want, Ciara. You're twenty-five years old and you've been going out with Billy for three years. He's asked you enough times to marry him. I was well married by your age."

Billy reminded Patricia of Sean, her husband, who died a few years after Ciara was born. She thought of Sean almost every day but more recently his image seemed to be fading.

In fact everything seemed to be shifting, moving and tilting so that even her memories were unreliable, and lately, Patricia had begun wondering what her life was all about. She had enough money. She had two beautiful daughters but she still felt restless.

Her two children were completely different.

Aisling her eldest daughter was fun and uncomplicated. She led a Bohemian life style and lived in Dublin. Ciara by comparison, was far less adventurous, and as much as Patricia loved them both she realised they didn't actually need her. She wasn't important to her children any more. They loved her but she wasn't integral to their complicated thoughts and privy to their dreams and aspirations.

Patricia needed something more. More adventure, excitement, a challenge - she wasn't sure what it was exactly - but she knew she needed something.

Ciara moved away from the window and turned her attention to the shelves. She had lost count of the times she had stocked the shelves. As a child it had been fun, as a teenager a chore, and now as an adult the shop was her life. Ciara loved it. She began turning the cans carefully so they were all facing neatly the same way, label to the front; mushroom soup, tomato, leek and potato.

Patricia smiled.

A few weeks later, Patricia standing at the same window, saw a white van park outside the shop and she watched with interest as three Indian men began to unload chairs, tables and big boxes.

She waited until she had served the last customer and the shop was empty, then she ran across the road. The eldest Indian man greeted her with a warm smile and a half bow.

Patricia blinked. His face was exotic.It was like soft, rich, dark toffee and his shining horse chestnut eyes seemed to glint in silent amusement. The sleeves of his white shirt were rolled up revealing smooth hairless arms and curiosity made her want to reach out and feel the texture of his skin. Instead she asked.

"When are you opening?"

"Next Friday - the eighth of December." He pronounced his words slowly and carefully, the vowels were carefully clipped. His lilting accent and deep voice made Patricia feel like she was wading in syrup.

"That's my birthday," Patricia said with surprise.

"I hope we will welcome you on our opening night." He waved his hand in the direction of the restaurant and tilted his head. "You are from the little shop?"

"Supermarket," she corrected. "My name's Patricia."

"I am Rajesh." His face broke into a smile revealing lopsided teeth. "Perhaps when we open I can buy some spices from you."

As he spoke, Patricia could smell the fragrant spices; gram masala, cumin, coriander, cloves, all of them so foreign and exciting. She would have to review her stock. She didn't want him to think this was some backwater sort of village with no stock.

One of the men placed a ladder against the front of the restaurant and began connecting wires to a fluorescent sign.

"I hope you call it something exotic like the Taj Mahal and not just the Curry House," she said, with a small laugh.

"It's called Jasmine, after my beautiful daughter," Rajesh said. He tilted his head. His palms were clasped and his fingertips placed together. Patricia thought it was the sweetest movement she had ever seen.

She imagined his tall, beautiful and elegant wife in a vibrantly coloured sari and a mini Jasmine just like her father with gleaming, excited eyes. She wondered if they would live in the small flat above the restaurant, as she and Sean had lived above the supermarket in the early days. She wanted him to have what she had once had, a happy family, and a home full of excitement and laughter.

"That's a pretty name," she said. Then from the corner of her eye she saw Jessica slip out of the pub and into the shop. "I have to go." And she ran back across the road.

"So, you're mixing with the foreigners then," Jessica announced, as Patricia slid behind the till.

She rolled chewing gum around her tongue, blew a small bubble, slapped two lemons onto the counter and flicked her long blond hair.

"I'm thinking of taking the family there for my birthday." Patricia smiled.

Jessica's face darkened. "But you always come to Murphy's."

"I know, but just for a change, I thought we'd try Jasmine's." The name rolled from her tongue like an old friend.

"There's nothing wrong with Murphy's, you know." Jessica dropped a few coins onto the counter and stormed out.

Patricia followed as far as the window, where she watched Jessica go into Billy's butcher's shop, village life, she thought. It was closing in on her.

After the early evening rush of customers subsided Ciara looked up from the till.

"We are going to Murphy's for your birthday like usual, aren't we?" Her face was as dark and ominous as the clouds outside.

Patricia shrugged. This was the problem with village life. It didn't take long for anything to get around. Why was everyone so stuck in their ways?

When her mother didn't reply, Ciara picked up a book beside the till that Patricia had been reading.

She read out the title, "A Passage to India." Then she picked up another one, "A Journey to Ithaca, Life in Modern India." She slammed them down. "Mammy, what's wrong? You've been to see Slumdog Millionaire twice and you've just read White Tiger, which if I'm not mistaken is another book about India. So what is all this?"

"I borrowed them from the library. I'm interested, Ciara. I need something more exciting than this shop and this village."

"It's been enough for you up to now. Are you bored? Do you want me to marry Billy and then you'll have a big wedding to plan? Or perhaps you want me to have babies so that you can fuss over some grandchildren?"

"No, of course not."

"So what is it then?"

"I don't know! Maybe…I want to be free."

"But you are free," Ciara answered.

"Not free, I mean…fulfilled. I think I want to be needed."

"Like as in a boyfriend?"

"No! No, Ciara. A boyfriend wouldn't solve anything. I need something more, something different." Patricia shook her head. There was no sense in trying to explain something she didn't understand herself.

Since Sean there had been a few men in her life but nothing serious. The last one had been married and it had been a disaster. Fortunately Ciara didn't know the whole story and that's the way it would stay.

Patricia knew she didn't want a relationship. Not

at the moment. It wouldn't be the solution to her restlessness. It was a different type of need. Something that Patricia had to fulfil inside herself - for her.

But Ciara's questioning only intensified her restlessness and Patricia spent the next few days hoping her mood of lethargy would pass and that the lifelessness that had seeped through the membrane of her soul would somehow disappear.

She felt hollow, as if the core of her inner-being was disintegrating. It was as if an invisible wind had gusted, knocking her off her destined path, setting her life's compass in dizzy turmoil.

She walked aimlessly in the cold beside the stark river bank, and she sat for hours at the back of the empty, silent church. Her world had shifted. It was out of sync, unbalanced and she felt unsure.

Each day Patricia watched as Rajesh settled into the building opposite. They were preparing for his opening night. Through the window she could feel his excitement as he decorated the restaurant with small red-tasseled lamps, pristine white table cloths, gleaming glasses and shining cutlery, while Patricia felt more and more cocooned in a trapped and silent world of her own.

Then one evening, in the glow of a damp December evening, looking at the cosy restaurant, Patricia began to have the stirrings of a vague idea. It began as a few snapshots. Pictures in her mind. It was an idea that was thrilling yet frightening and another type of anxiety filled her soul.

A few days later, Patricia was filled with energy and determination, so she went up to Dublin on the train and met her eldest daughter for lunch.

Aisling looked so much like Sean that when she saw her clear grey-blue eyes and dark hair, she felt a pang of loss so deep, she almost cried.

To divert her wandering mind she told Aisling about the new restaurant and over lunch they discussed Patricia's looming birthday. When Patricia voiced her ideas Aisling saw her mother's face shine with excitement. She was stunned by her mother's radiant beauty and when Patricia smiled it was with confidence. Her decision was made. It was as if a veil had been lifted from her face. Her green eyes sparkled and even her freckles seemed to glow like gold dust on her cheeks.

Her daughter Aisling had always behaved unconventionally. She craved excitement and flirted with a risqué lifestyle.

"Ciara won't be pleased," Aisling said finally.

"It will be good for her," Patricia replied with a reckless laugh.

On the morning of her fifty-fifth birthday Patricia woke early. She was excited and nervous. But more importantly she was determined to enjoy her day whatever the outcome and whatever anyone in the village thought. She felt she was finally putting her life's compass back on course.

That evening when she opened the door of Jasmine's, a rush of exhilaration flashed through her veins as rich aromas from the kitchen danced in her soul, waking the dormant senses in her body. Herbs, seasoning, spices: cardamom, cloves, fennel seeds, ginger, garlic and chillies. They seeped into and under her skin, causing goose pimples to rise on her arms

124

and a ripple of anticipation to flood through her body.

Rajesh was dressed traditionally in white embroidered cotton tunic and trousers. She thought he looked like an exotic Maharaja. At first he frowned in bewilderment then he rushed over with his hand held out.

"Forgive me. I didn't recognise you, Patricia. Then I saw your lovely green eyes and your beautiful…" He swept his eyes approvingly over her body.

She wore a deep violet sari, with matching bracelets and bangles, and from her neck hung an intricately designed silver necklace. Her auburn hair was wound up on top of her head where loose tendrils were escaping around her pixie-shaped ears, and he gasped in delight when he saw the elaborate henna tattoos that covered her hands.

He was about to speak when the door flew open and Ciara appeared with Billy.

Ciara's normal frown turned into a look of complete disbelief and a sharp cry escaped her lips.

"Mammy? What on earth…? What have you done to yourself?"

Billy began to giggle.

"Shut up, Billy." Ciara thumped his arm.

"Please, here is the table you reserved. Perhaps I can invite you to a glass of wine?" Rajesh ushered Patricia to the best table in the window.

"Have you gone nuts?" Ciara whispered loudly as she sat down beside her mother. "Why have you done this? Are you trying to embarrass me?"

"I need a change, Ciara." Patricia was determined Ciara wouldn't ruin the evening.

"But? Where did you get this from?" She pulled on the sari and was surprised by the softness of its touch.

"Aisling bought it for me. It's my birthday present."

"I might have guessed that hippy would be involved - and these tattoos on your hand?"

"They wash off." Patricia reached out to touch Ciara's hand but Ciara pulled it quickly away and placed it in her lap just as Rajesh returned.

He placed three glasses and a bottle of red wine on the table, then he added dishes of Poppadoms, Onion Bhajis, and Samosas.

"This…" he said, placing a small dish on the table, "is Paneer pieces dipped in masala and gram flour batter and deep-fried in oil, all with our compliments." He tilted his head and smiled.

"Thank you, Rajesh. Where's your wife and Jasmine, the daughter who you named the restaurant after? I'd love to meet them."

Rajesh shook his head. "Unfortunately they were all killed in the Kashmir earthquake in 2005. This restaurant is a tribute to my daughter and all the unfulfilled lives that were lost that day. They are with God now but I'm sure they are all here with us in spirit." His brown eyes filled with tears as he turned to greet a small crowd who surged in, bringing an icy December wind that swept through Patricia's body.

She knew then, without any doubt, that she had done the right thing. She wanted to make a difference. She guessed it wouldn't be the right moment to tell Ciara that she was going to India in the New Year.

Her ticket was booked.

Stari Most

Jasminka was walking back from the market and had just turned the corner into her street when she stopped in shock.

One of the boys on the Old Bridge was exactly like Zoran Pejanovic had been twenty years ago.

Was it his walk or confident smile?

The Japanese tourists readied their cameras, Germans leaned over the rail, and women covered their mouths as, one by one, the boys competed and threw themselves twenty-one feet into the icy river below.

The girls giggled just as Jasminka had done all those years ago when Zoran flirted with her. She remembered him teasing her as if it were yesterday.

'What would you do if I couldn't swim?' he asked.

'I'd save you,' she replied.

'Would you miss me if I drowned?'

'I'd jump in and rescue you,' she replied.

'And ruin that pretty dress?' His eyes lingered on her pert breasts

'I'd remove that first, of course,' she replied giggling.

But that was a long time ago, before the war of 1992.

She had been a young girl then, just out of her

127

teens. Zoran and his family had been neighbours and they had lived in this very street. It had been a time when all the boys had wrestled playfully to prove their manhood. They had jumped from the Stari Most, played football together and shared thick rich coffee in the square.

Only the war changed all that.

Now, she stood under the awning of a tourist shop, placed her shopping bags at her feet and watched the 'jumpers,' young men strutting in shorts gaining the attention of the crowd before diving into the Neretva River below.

There were lots of tourists. It was a good day for trade. Jasminka knew they came from cruise ships moored in Dubrovnik, visiting Mostar before going on to Medjugorje, the apparition site of Our Lady.

Jasminka had been a nurse during the war. She had seen enough to know there was nothing but the emptiness of death. Stark, painful, traumatic. Rarely was it peaceful or was there ever a miracle. It was just death.

"Que peligrosa! Madre mia!" A woman beside her gasped.

The young Zoran-looking boy had dived off the bridge.

Jasminka replied in broken and hesitating English. It was the only foreign language she knew.

"In July we have the Bridge Jumping competition. They are practicing," she explained.

The Spanish woman nodded encouragingly, and pleased she understood, Jasminka continued.

"It's an age-old tradition. Each jumper becomes a hero when they throw themselves from the bridge."

The Spanish woman peered over the wall to the river below, to where a boy, with long reaching strokes, swam to the river bank.

"The bridge is beautiful."

Jasminka remembered when the Old Bridge had been completely destroyed, now the crescent-shaped, single-arched structure looked perfect. "They rebuilt it. The Old Bridge, the Stari Most, joins the east and the west of Mostar, separating Muslims from Christians, uniting and dividing."

"Mostar is a beautiful place but so many buildings are destroyed?" The Spanish woman's brown eyes surveyed the scene around her.

If only she knew, thought Jasminka.

The war had changed everything and everyone. Buildings were ravaged, as were the people. Empty windows staring like sightless eyes. Streets bombed and reduced to rubble, crumbled like the lives of those who had lived there.

"After the war there was a five-year plan to rebuild the city, to regenerate and restore the historic old town," Jasminka replied, remembering how she had spent the war nursing the injured in a basement cellar. It had been converted to a makeshift hospital. It was fetid and smelt of blood. Children lay on bloodied stretchers and there was no medication and no sterilisation.

She nursed many, including those she loved, friends, neighbours and even her family. Her father's face had been partially blown away by shrapnel. Naively, she thought he could be stitched up, until she saw the gaping hole in his stomach and her hands were filled with his warm blood.

"These shops have so much character," the Spanish woman replied.

Jasminka nodded.

She wanted to tell the foreigner that two of the shops were owned by men who had once vied for her attention. They had both wanted to marry her.

Growing up they had been best friends but they hadn't spoken to each other for over twenty years.

From her sheltered vantage point she watched Zoran hobble out from his shop manipulating his worn crutches as if they were an extension of his body. His missing leg belied the strength of his muscular body, his strong upper torso and broad shoulders. As he served a tourist, she saw Zoran's dark hair was as unkempt as his rakish smile.

She remembered how flies had gorged on open wounds, operating areas had not been sanitised and as a result many people had ended with amputations. Only the strong had survived.

"That poor man," whispered the Spanish woman. "So many casualties."

Two doors down from where Zoran's stood, Mile Ivanović emerged from the darkness of his shop.

Mile's art studio was on the ground floor of a narrow three-story house with green shuttered windows and potted colourful geraniums hanging from wrought iron balconies. The flowers added an air of cosmopolitanism to the street and tourists often stopped to take pictures.

It would be hard for them, Jasminka thought, to imagine the ravaged bomb blasts that destroyed the street, leaving crushed stone that had once been their homes.

Mile shaded his eyes from the brightness of the sun. He was a giant of a man, wide, tall and with sparse grey hair and a thick white bushy moustache.

"I bought a painting from that man." The Spaniard raised a covered package for Jasminka to see. "He wrapped it so carefully for me to take back to Madrid."

"Mile has always been thoughtful."

She remembered him as a boy. He was quieter than most and a deep thinker. He had spent hours carving intricate patterns in pieces of wood. He sketched on anything he could find, using hard lumps of charcoal, turning plain and ugly into interesting and beautiful.

When the stronger boys had jumped off the bridge, Mile had been more concerned about the shapes they formed, the curves of their bodies and the patterns created in the rippling water below.

"He was always very artistic."

The art studio had once been Mile's father's tailor shop where, as a child, Jasminka had taken clothes for repair.

Once when she had been very young, her eyes had locked with the young Mile, and her heart had fluttered. Mile had never been particularly handsome but there was something calming in his deep-set eyes that made her realise he was both reliable and honourable.

Then, when the war was over, and his father gone, Mile had rebuilt the shop and helped others in his street to repair theirs.

But Mile had never helped his boyhood friend Zoran.

Mile was another casualty of war but he had been lucky. Unlike his father, three brothers, two uncles and his nephew, who were all buried side by side on the hillside on the outskirts of town, Mile had survived. He had spent years trying to trace his sister and her husband who were still missing and now assumed to be in a mass grave in East Bosnia, part of the mass genocide that had taken place in Srebrenica.

A German tourist paused at Mile's studio and pointed to a painting hanging in the doorway. Mile lifted it down before disappearing inside with the foreigner who began pulling a wallet from his back pocket.

Jasminka and the Spanish lady stood lost in their thoughts watching as Zoran wrapped a colourful shawl. It would be unpacked and worn in Osaka, Hamburg or Madrid. Or perhaps the tourist had bought one of his jewel-handled daggers or Turkish-styled pewter tea-set.

"It says here, the bridge was destroyed during the war in 1992." The Spanish woman read from a guide book.

Yes, thought Jasminka, when anger, resentment and recriminations raged. It had been shelled mercilessly from the hills surrounding the town. One invading force after the other had destroyed her streets and her family.

"The bridge was rebuilt after the war and crowned heads of Europe attended the opening in 2004." The Spanish woman nodded as she read aloud. She seemed impressed. And Jasminka remembered a time when scaffolding had protected the bridge and a white flag fluttered in the wind.

The war had been an enigma to her. She had never been interested in politics and she was confused with the various armies; the Yugoslav People's Army, the Serbian forces, the Bosnian army and Croatian extremists. They had all changed sides and allegiances during the various stages of the war that had lasted until 1996.

All she knew was that everything became more confused as neighbours turned on each other, friends fought on opposite sides, and the cruelty and bombings intensified.

Then there were reports of genocide, mass graves, young men and boys taken into forests and shot, and unspeakable injustices done to women.

Jasminka shivered with fear under the awning of the tourist shop.

Why had the UN Forces taken so long to help? Was it, as Mile always said, because Bosnia was a pretty alpine country and had no oil?

"Are you alright?" The Spanish woman reached out her hand and touched Jasminka's arm. There was empathy in the stranger's dark eyes. "It must be hard for you…"

Many houses that were off the tourist route were still bullet-riddled, and some still stood as burnt-out shells. They were a testament to the tragedy that had besieged Mostar. She couldn't help the memories that sprung up and overwhelmed her. They engulfed her normally positive spirit and today Jasminka had caught a glimpse of her past, and she remembered the young men who had once loved her.

This won't do, she thought, and with a sudden burst of optimistic energy, she said: "Today I am cooking Burek,"

The Spanish woman looked bemused so Jasminka explained.

"Pies with thin flat pastry filled with salty cheese - pita od sira, or minced meat." She wasn't sure if the Spanish woman understood her English or her Bosnian but she said that she would prepare them in a large pan and cut them into portions after baking.

"They are my husband's favourites." And suddenly, distraught with her memories, Jasminka had an urge to be with him.

She picked up the shopping bags at her feet and nodded at the foreigner.

"Vaya con Dios," the Spanish woman said.

Jasminka walked slowly, but her mind continued to whirl in reminiscence.

During the war she had nursed both Zoran and Mile.

Zoran had the skills of a survivor and had left the hospital on crutches and a face filled with angry determination. When the streets were bombed and the buildings were desecrated, Zoran found out which owners lived or died. He was an opportunist and even on one leg he would not be defeated. He controlled a group of boys and the black market. After the war and during the rebuilding of the town, he offered the widow of his shop half its original value, shrewdly promising to pay her its full worth, if her husband returned. The widow was Mile's Aunt.

Now, as she passed his shop, Jazminka saw Zoran's worn face. It showed none of the charm he had once commanded. She knew, as did half of the people in the town, he was unhappily married. It was said, he spent most nights paying young girls in the poorer part of town but Jasminka didn't listen to gossip, just like the gossip that said she had broken his heart all those years ago.

In the art studio Mile looked up and smiled.

"You sold another painting of Stari Most, I suppose," she smiled.

Mile shrugged and looked at all the similar paintings that covered the wall.

"They all love the Old Bridge. They took my favourite. The one I hung up with no frame. But I'll just have to do another," he sighed theatrically. From this angle, Jasminka couldn't see Mile's withered left arm, caught in a bomb blast, that dangled at his side.

"Not again…" There was a giggle from the far side of the room, and in the light of the window a pretty girl sat curled up on a thick cushion with a sketch pad on her knee.

"Mama," Katya called, her deep blue eyes alive with youth. "Look! What do you think of this painting? I'm sick of that bridge! I wanted to do something different." She sat surrounded by paints. Her fingers covered in multiple colours.

At sixteen Katya looked like her mother. They shared the same intense dark eyes, wide mouth and pert nose. Jasminka's sister had been brutally raped during the war and had died in child birth. Jasminka and Mile had raised Katya as their own child.

"That's very pretty…"

Katya was studying fashion design and soon she would go to University in Sarajevo. Jasminka knew that when she left, it would be another loss in their lives but this time not a permanent one. Katya would

come home during the holidays, unlike so many of
their family, who would never return.

Dublin 1832
The Golden Icon - Prelude

Death hangs over us like a shroud from the minute we are born to the day we die. It is only through the Grace of God that we are allowed to live long enough to realise our dreams. That is, if you believe in God, like Kate McCarron did.

That was where her opinion differed to that of her cousin, Dr Patrick McCarron, an atheist and physician who believed that the most interesting part of life is death and without it, he argued, we wouldn't know what life was about. It was only through discovery and dissection of the body that we can learn about the soul, the spiritual life and the eternal life.

Kate had been born into inescapable poverty. Born never to be her own mistress and expected to die young. Now, she was holding the hand of her dying cousin, the sister of Dr Patrick McCarron and her best friend.

Their shared bedroom was sparse with only wooden twin beds and twin crucifixes at their heads, and a rickety table between them. A lone candle burned the back of her eyes; red and raw with tears and tiredness. Her throat was dry and she coughed into a rag. Her mood was darkening in pace with the sinking bleak day, and hope was being extinguished in front of her eyes.

Typhus would soon claim her as its next victim. As it had her parents, a year ago and only a month apart, and her twin brothers shortly after that.

Kate now lived at the mercy of her ambitious Uncle, Rebecca's father and a staunch supporter of the Catholic Church. Kate hated him and the Church, just as much as she hated her cousin Patrick.

Rebecca kicked her legs feebly. "Don't let them…," she mumbled. She took a shivering breath that sucked strength from her emaciated body. "Promise me?"

Kate kissed the skeletal fingers of her friend's hand.

They had discussed this many times in the past few months. How often had they heard Patrick saying he wanted to dissect a body with the blood still flowing warm?

Now, as the end drew near, Rebecca's fear gathered momentum and the intensity of her voice sliced across the dimly lit room and fear gathered in her soul.

"Don't let him find me…"

"He won't. I promise."

It was the promise of a naïve sixteen year old with no money, no friends and a powerful cousin intent on discovery.

A man who valued death over life. A man whose desire for medical knowledge exceeded all rational and religious teachings, and a man who feared nothing and no-one. Not even God.

Kate was hot and she felt faint in the sick confines of the room. She smoothed strands of lank hair from Rebecca's damp forehead and coughed. She too felt feverish.

Her floor-length skirt was pleated into the waistband of the bodice and held out with a starched cotton petticoat. Her hair was parted in the centre, curls looped and knotted were braided at the crown of her head.

Her cousin had once been young and beautiful. They had grown up together, in the countryside working on the farms and the agricultural lands owned by the Protestant gentry. Kate remembered the day they stood with the crowds, corn ripening under the warm sunlight, and their youthful hearts filled with determination.

They had cheered for O'Connell.

Rumour had it that the Pope was sending financial aid and that the Irish Rebellion would be funded. This gave them hope and they vowed they would escape poverty and the tyrannical rule of the British.

A year later, Kate's scheming Uncle had increased his finances and moved with his two children to the capital.

Kate had only been reunited with Rebecca following the death of her own parents. Now she was about to lose her too, and the dreams they once shared were being extinguished in this dark and dingy room.

"I'll never be with God, if he, if they…" Rebecca's mumbled words expired with a shudder.

She fell silent. It was her last breath.

Kate coughed. She wiped the perspiration from her forehead. All air had been sucked from the room, and replaced with peace from the rasping breath and beating of fear in her best friend's heart.

It was over.

Kate had no tears left. All she had was hollowness in her heart and the burning determination of her rash promise.

She wondered how she could keep it.

***

Prospects Cemetery was well guarded with four stone towers, one in each corner of the burial ground, built as a precaution and defence.

Inside the four towers, huddled against the cold wind, hired men watched with tired eyes. They spoke in whispers, scanning the darkness for a sign of movement.

Body snatching was big business and there was money in the proceeds. The Catholic Church was determined to protect the hearts and souls of the deceased from the surgical instruments of the atheist radicals. Rumour had it, that in the north, bodies were taken as far as Glasgow and transported in barrels across the sea. In Dublin the Royal College of Surgeons also paid a high price for a fresh dead body.

Today there had been many funerals including an Italian priest on a mission from the Pope, a revolutionary shot by the British, and many casualties of the rapidly spreading Typhus.

Fresh earthy mounds lay in various corners of the cemetery, occasionally highlighted by a half-moon that dodged intermittently behind the fast moving clouds.

Connor McGivern had been paid well. His instructions had been clear. Now he watched a rival group to his left, darting between the graves. His friend Ted stood to his side and they swapped a knowing look. It would be immediate death if they were caught. The men in the watchtowers were armed. They were paid to kill.

So they waited.

They watched three dark figures as they worked quietly over a new mound of earth. They were quick. Their shovels soundlessly flicking the earth to one side.

Connor signalled with the nod of his head. Their timing must be perfect.

As the moon disappeared Connor ran toward the men and the open grave. The three men were so involved in their work they hadn't even the sense to leave a man on duty to watch and they were caught by surprise.

The first man, standing waist high in the grave looked up, raised his shovel swinging it toward Connor's face. Connor ducked and, grabbing a handful of earth, he threw it in the man's eyes.

Behind him, Ted kicked the second man in the groin and, turning adeptly, punched the third man in the windpipe.

In the distance a dog barked. There was a shout. The men from the watchtower had been alerted.

Connor's timing couldn't have been more perfect. As the man in the grave wiped the dirt from his eyes Connor grabbed the package. It was smaller and heavier than he anticipated and he stumbled. Regaining his footing he scrambled to his feet and began to run, darting between the grave stones, tombs and Celtic crosses. Ted followed, heading for their planned escape route. Over his shoulder he heard a rifle shot.

At the edge of the cemetery, under the shadow of an old fir tree they paused for breath. The dog's barking began to recede. Connor panted heavily. He imagined the three men had been caught. God had been on their side tonight.

Connor tucked the package inside his cassock. Secretly, he didn't care about the church, or the package or the rumours that the Pope was sending Italian troops to fight against the British Protestants. All he cared about was money. His mother was ill and needed medicine and he had been paid above the odds to get the package.

Whatever the package contained, it was heavy, and it was a burden he couldn't wait to be rid of.

***

Kate had been lying for hours in the darkness gazing up at the ceiling. She imagined a colourful heaven with winged angels and Rebecca smiling, running through golden fields of corn, calling her to follow.

That afternoon, at the funeral, her tears had fallen easily. Now she had a headache and was exhausted. She had kept her promise. Rebecca was buried in Prospects Cemetery. Kate's Uncle had arranged it, and since then, there had been a stream of visitors to her Uncle's study below and she had listened to their muffled voices.

After dinner, two men of the cloth had arrived. Although this wasn't unusual, these men had looked dishevelled and muddy, and her Uncle's usual worried expression had changed to excitement and his rodent eyes gleamed. She was used to the coming and going of people at all hours but, this evening, it was different. He had sent her to her room, all thoughts of his daughter's death and her funeral, instantly forgotten.

Kate had been curious. She had tiptoed carefully down the creaking staircase to peer through a crack in the door. The men were huddled together. Then she saw her Uncle place something into the safe in the back of the room, money changed hands, and after a few minutes they left, leaving Kate to scurry quickly up the stairs.

A few minutes earlier, she had heard her cousin's horse arrive, then his heavy footsteps inside the house. Now, her Uncle, a religious man who rarely had time for heathens, and his son Patrick who had a severe dislike for the hypocrisy of the church, were locked in the study like two predators.

The only common attribute they had was their greed.

Kate coughed and tossed back the worn blanket. Her feet were cold on the wooden boards. She threw a cloak over her nightdress and cursed as she snagged her toe on a nail. She walked cautiously down the stairs and paused on the bottom step.

A yellow glow of candlelight shone from under the door and she could hear angry voices. Holding her hand against the wall, careful not to trip, she placed an ear to the door.

"Medical science? You'll never discover how the body works," her Uncle's voice was agitated.

"And if I found a cure for Typhus?"

143

Her Uncle taunted him. "You're mad. Our body and soul belongs to Christ, as one entity, not to go to heaven separately. You're a heathen and a fool."

Patrick's words were muffled as his boots struck the wooden floor.

Kate prepared to run for the stairs. But his next words caused her to falter.

"It belongs to the Cause. Not to your Church."

"A deal is a deal, Patrick. It's against my principles but she's yours if you stay quiet."

There was scuffling of footsteps. They had moved farther inside the room. Whispered voices. Suddenly, quick, heavy footsteps came toward her.

"I'll be back - to collect."

Kate ran.

The door was flung open. At the top of the stairs she paused in the shadows. Her heart pounding. Patrick stormed from the room and slammed out of the front door.

She wiped beads of perspiration from her forehead. If she was discovered she would face the wrath of her Uncle and another beating. She heard her Uncle's boots. She was too frightened to move.

A long shadow cast over the wall and her Uncle appeared in the doorway. He hesitated. She thought he saw her, and she was about to move forward into the light, but then he turned and in three strides he was at the front door. He slammed and locked it behind him.

Kate slumped down against the wall and sat on the step. All she could hear was the rapid beating of her heart. Perspiration was trickling from her forehead. When she felt quite sure it was safe she ventured back down stairs.

The big candle was burning so she guessed he wouldn't be long. She knew the key was hidden in a drawer. She had discovered it one day when she had been sent in to clean. It was still there. She moved the tapestry to one side and the rusted key turned easily.

Inside was a bulky, dirty cloth tied with frayed thin rope. It was twice the length of her hand and heavy. She walked over to the candlelight to look more closely at the knots. It had been carelessly tied as if someone had hurriedly examined the contents.

She tugged the knot but was distracted.

Her Uncle's workbench, normally covered with various bibles and other Christian books, was now covered by a mummy-looking figure, wrapped in cloth, a life-size replica of the package in her hand.

Gripping the parcel in her left hand Kate walked to the work bench. Her heart beating wildly. She traced the outline with the tips of her fingers, recognising the familiar shape of a body. Tentatively she reached out with her right hand and pulled back the material. The fabric fell away and in the yellow candlelight staring back at her was Rebecca's dead face.

Kate gasped and took a step back.

The cloth from the figure in her hand fell away and when she looked down she saw a Golden Icon, and the perfectly sculptured face of the Madonna. Her serenity and beauty was breathtaking and in stark contrast with her dead friend's waxy corpse.

Outside there was the rattle of a wagon, a shout and a horse whinnied.

Instinctively Kate ran.

145

Her Uncle may be a man of the church but his fury was like no other.

But it was Patrick who frightened her the most. He wanted a warm dead body and he didn't care how he got it.

It wasn't the first time in her life that Kate understood the fear of God.

Upstairs, she coughed into a rag, tugged on her boots and threw her outdoor cloak around her shoulders. She slipped the heavy Golden Icon into her blouse. She must get it to the Rebels.

The front door opened. There were heavy footsteps and a shout of alarm.

In one movement, she prised open her bedroom window and without a backward glance she slid outside onto the neighbour's roof.

They would follow her. She knew there would be no escape.

But she would die fighting. Fighting for the Cause. Just as she and Rebecca had always dreamed.

White Shadow

It had been his intention to sit in the shade of the terrace, avoiding the harsh Spanish sun and wait for his coffee, but a shard of sunlight sliced across his face. It parted the middle of his forehead, splitting his narrow bent nose, his jutting chin, and dividing his chest and gentiles like a meat cleaver. He imagined a sharp rotating blade neatly slicing him in half.

Only one half of him in the sun. His two enquiring eyes, two ears, two nostrils and his half smile separated into dark and light.

The waiter, dressed immaculately in pressed black trousers and cotton shirt, places the white cup and saucer on the table. He has grey hair and dark skin and his attention is diverted by the arrival of a pretty girl. He smiles when she sits at the opposite table.

The man follows the waiter's gaze.

She has a heart-shaped face, long dark hair and blue eyes. Her skin is pale like cold marble. She tosses the daily newspaper onto the table, crosses her bare legs and orders orange juice. Like the waiter, she too, is Spanish. She stabs the paper with her finger when the waiter reappears with her juice. The ice rattles like a skeleton in the glass.

"Has visto? Have you seen this?" she says with familiarity, as though she knows the waiter. He pauses and looks over her shoulder. "The killer could strike again, there's been one victim in a different

147

city, each week for two months. He's a serial killer and he's working his way around the country." Her voice is light, but her tone strained and her eyes worried.

The waiter studies the black and white print.

"No te preocupes." The waiter's voice is deep, his response measured. "Don't worry! Valencia is a long way from Malaga. He would need a fast car to be here today–"

"He might have driven through the night. He could easily be here…"

The man adds sugar to his black coffee and stirs slowly. He is exhausted, there are black circles under his eyes and he smothers a yawn.

The shadow moves on the terrace. The man shifts his chair, so that the line of sun and shade remains in equal halves across his body. He enjoys the heat on one side and the cool shadow on the other, dividing him, slicing him into two.

What, he wondered, would happen if I were cut open?

What sort of person would I be?

Divided exactly into equal, symmetrical, mirrored halves. There would be subtle differences, of course, like the heart beating rhythmically on the left. Perhaps his soul would be lodged on the right, to provide balance to his divided being.

Good and bad - equally balanced?

His Ying and his Yang dissected by a slice of sunlight.

Not torn or ripped, but carefully cut and his blood like a ribbon of fine red silk. He would be exposed yet protected, tough yet vulnerable, both wise and naive.

Who would he be?

Where would his brain lie? Divided in two. Indecisive, torn, unsure?

Reason versus illogic thoughts. Love versus hate, calm versus chaos.

A white Nissan Micra toots its horn and distracted he looks up.

It parks in a narrow gap blocking the dark alley to the cobbled streets of the old quarter. It is against the law to park there but the driver, a colourfully dressed woman with a mane of blond hair, locks the door and skips quickly into the bakery.

The man toys with the salt cellar and pepper pot. He mixes an equal amount of grain in his palm; white and black. Then he tosses them on the floor and wipes his hand on his trousers.

He regards the girl. She is engrossed in her story about the killer in Valencia. She leans across the table, holding her long hair back from her face, periodically sipping her juice without distraction. Her head moves slowly as she reads the words like an old typewriter with a carriage return.

The white shadow creates heat down the left half of his body but he doesn't move.

Instead, he admires the perfect symmetry down the long contour of his figure and feels a wave of warmth, or is it inspiration, desire or longing?

He notes the contrast of the dark half, but the two sides are delicately balanced, as precarious as the scales of justice; weakness balancing strength. He tilts his waist slowly to the left, then returns to the centre before tilting to the right, balancing the strong sunny side, supporting the vulnerable dark side.

Hope encourages doubt and despair, and his mood lightens momentarily then it evaporates like a fine forest mist lifting toward the early morning heaven, swirling into eternity and disappearing into nothingness.

There is no hope. It is gone.

The girl looks up. Their eyes meet and she smiles quickly before returning her attention to her reading.

The waiter reappears and covers a table with a white paper tablecloth, clipping its sides against the swelling breeze. He is preparing for lunch.

If, the man reasons, my brain is divided but my heart is whole, would I experience emptiness and fullness or only loneliness?

Where is reason?

Where is love, hate, courage and fear, worry and confidence?

Would he be a shadow of himself?

Who is he now?

Time moves and heals, giving strength and uniting. A heart beating to the soulful rhythm of reason, common sense and simple pleasure.

Time.

He must be patient.

The waiter lays cutlery and when he disappears inside the cafe, the man reaches over and picks up a knife. He runs his finger along the edge of the blade. He imagines thinly sliced slivers of emotion severed on a platter of grey matter. Emotions caressing, pulsating like red blood-filled beating arteries, drained by black veins; arterial routes leading to despair.

If he stood up, would he fall apart or would the other half heal? Would it be an invisible presence, a missing amputated part or more like an absent twin or a guardian angel?

Would he listen with only one ear, see with one eye, speak with a divided tongue? Taste only half the flavours, smell half the aromas, understand only half a language?

He turns the knife in his hands. He rotates it. First in the shade and then in the sunlight. It flickers and reflects on the girl's face like a shining beacon and she looks up.

He smiles. "Sorry," he says.

She shrugs. "Have you seen this?" She jabs the paper with her finger. "What sort of man could do this?"

He shakes his head. He imagines her face cut into two halves. Two enquiring eyes, two small ears, two nostrils and one mouth with half of a whole smile.

"What sort of savage is he?" The girl turns the page and the man sees more images. Black and white pictures. Silhouettes of a ravaged body.

"He cuts them in two," she says.

The man imagines hearing half a sound, half a meaning or half a truth. Would he be wiser in his ignorance or more comfortable in his bliss? Tasting only half of life's flavours, never satisfied, never sated. Would it cause him to yearn for more? Yearning for the invisible, missing and longing for his other half?

His manicured nails are white against his tanned skin.

Imagine touching with five fingers instead of ten. Feathery light fingers, a dark and heavy hand. Letting go, holding on; grasping and pulling, pushing and repelling. Struggling and suffocating.

Able bodies that carry the burden of life would carry only half the weight. Would they carry only half the problem?

The woman in the Nissan Micra runs back to her car. She throws a bag of bread onto the seat and drives off, unblocking the shadowed alley that stands like a gaping toothless, mirthless smile.

The waiter appears with glasses and the girl calls to him.

"He cuts off their hair," she says. "He hacks it off with a serrated-edged knife that he uses to cut her down the middle."

The waiter pauses holding a glass midway to the table.

"He's sick!" his voice is baritone.

"He's dangerous!" The girl replies in her light and feathery voice.

The man imagines their vocal tones as notes on a music score. White paper, black notes, quivers, quavers, staccato and alto.

He hears their piercing screams.

The music of their vocal cords is like a rumble of thunder across the sea in a tropical storm. The splash of one wave, a lonely monotone, no depth, no bass, no percussion. Raindrops in a storm, cascading until the deafening crescendo. A tempest receding, like half an unspoken truth, is it better to hear nothing at all?

"She was the fifth." The girl points at the black

152

and white portrait of a smiling woman.

"No te preocupes," the waiter responds. "Do not worry. They will catch him soon.

The sun shifts, moving with dexterity and grace, unnoticeable, so the man is encased totally in shadow. When he looks again, he sees that the girl is now divided in two. Half of her lies in shadow, the other in soft sunlight. He tilts his waist so the line divides her exactly in two, first one way, and then the other.

"Do you think I should cut my hair?" She pulls it to one side, over her shoulder. It is straight, black and glistens blue. "What do you think?" She looks up and meets his gaze. "Should I cut it?"

"I think your hair is beautiful."

She smiles shyly. She is flirting with him.

"No," replies the man thoughtfully, "Do not cut it."

He wonders how easily she made conversation. How quickly she asked his opinion. How safe she feels. Sitting in the shadow he is no longer a man divided. His heartbeat and his soul are joined and tethered. Two separated sides united by a slice of hope, a ray of invisible lightness like dissolvable stitches or transparent adhesive sticking him together. Piecing together his pain, his thoughts and his conscience.

His body morphs and his two halves have become one. He is whole again. He knows who he is.

You are my light she had said. She had flirted with him too.

You are my other half he replied.

He feels the light and smells its humid warmth. He remembers her in his arms, believing her to be nature's wholesome gift, her warm body filled with passion. He remembers the rotting vegetation on the damp forest floor. They were both equally needy. It was over as quick as a slice.

He trails the knife along the length of his index finger and remembers the hurt, the loss and the anger.

"Are you OK?" The girl's voice is concerned. Her brows are knotted together. Her hair is divided by an exact middle parting.

He nods and offers her half a smile.

"You're not from around here, are you?"

He shakes his head. His coffee has grown cold. He glances across to the alleyway that seems to beckon him. Drawing him like a magnet toward its gaping, tempting mouth.

"Do you think he plans to kill them? Or do you think it's random?" Her voice draws him toward her. She sucks her juice through the straw and he watches the orange disappear from the tall glass.

"You think too much! Don't read any more," the waiter replies, instead of the man. It is the waiter who goes to the girl and attempts to close the newspaper. He takes it from her grasp, undoing the tight grip of her white fingers.

"I must read it," she says. "I must be prepared."

She snatches at it, but it rips and tears.

"Don't think about these things. Don't dwell on sad things or you will draw in negative energy."

She looks at him. Dark eyes against pale skin.

"Do killers sit in the sun like ordinary people or do they sit at home in the dark behind drawn blinds, lurking in the shadows?"

"They are like us," the man responds, "just like

us."

The girl and the waiter both turn to him. He continues "They sit. They wait, and they watch. They consider random versus predictability. They are opportunists."

The waiter nods in agreement.

They have all bonded in understanding and by mutual consent they comprehend the enemy.

The man pays his bill.

The girl pulls her purse from her bag. On the table is the torn newspaper and the black and white images of a dead girl's face.

He wants to say I knew her. I loved her. She was once my girlfriend.

Instead he stands. He pockets the knife and wipes a fleck of blood from his finger onto his dark trousers.

"Are you walking to the old quarter?" The girl pushes back her chair at the same time.

"Yes."

"Will you walk with me?"

He tilts his head in agreement.

"You can't be too careful," she says, tucking her hand into the nook of the stranger's arm.

He yawns. He has been awake all night. His back aches from the car journey.

At the edge of the terrace a black cat pauses mid stride, as if to make sure they will follow. It crosses in front of them heading to the dark, open-mouthed alleyway. The cat's sleek fur shining, like the girl's hair hanging down her back. They walk in the bright, heat of the sun into the cold shadow of the gaping, toothless, passageway.

Three Days Dead

I am a healthy 58 year-old male.

This morning I had a pain in my head. I remember falling. Now I am dead. I am not shocked, horrified, or mortified. I cannot be. I no longer exist.

Now, I am an observer of people. I see my friends, my family and strangers. I am in limbo, like Jesus in the garden, three days afterwards and before he ascended into heaven. When he appeared to Doubting Thomas and he still had the wounds in the palm of his hands.

The difference is, is that I am not the son of God.

No-one will see me or feel my presence. They do not know that I have three days to see them, to watch their lives, to hear them speak, to understand their ways.

It's like a one-way mirror and I am the one doing all the looking.

Walls hold no barriers. I am like a wisp of air that can pass unseen and unnoticed except that sometimes, some people may feel a slight chill, or a shiver in their spine or, perhaps even a fleeting awareness of a change in atmosphere. That is me as I hover around them.

These people are attuned with the dead.

I slide between walls, under doors, through houses, swooping over rooftops. I cross angry seas and vast oceans, flying without fear and without weight.

My senses are honed. I am twisting and turning on the earth's currents, floating on the world's pulsating breath; in and out, in and out.

In Africa they sleep, in America they dream, and in Japan they dance. Time is immaterial. Nothingness stretches into infinity. In out, in out, in out. I am ebbing and flowing on a tide of humanity, relying on my conscience and my senses to guide me.

But my family is my priority. They are my loss.

My wife Suzie is weak and totally dependent on me.

Ben, my son is a recovering drug addict.

And Frances, my precious daughter, lives with a Polish man and has two illegitimate children.

But they all rely on me.

They need me. I am the helm in the stormy waters of their lives.

I slip though the walls of my home. I am my invisible self. My family are gathered around the kitchen table, their faces ashen and eyes downcast. They barely look at each other.

I view them from the ceiling, from the far end of the room, and from immediately beside them, guided by an inner radar, a sixth sense, and an unthinking stance. I am everywhere. I am nowhere. I am unable to reach out and to hold them for one final time. Unable to clasp them in my arms and unable to feel their breath on my cheek.

I am me but not me. I am a part of me. I am like an action, a reflex action, a reaction to my needs, like swallowing, blinking or breathing. Only I am not breathing now.

Suzie leans on her arms spilling slow, mournful

tears and she stems their flow by plugging a tissue into the corner of her red eyes.

How will she live without me?

Ben hovers uncertainly behind her, shifting his stance from one foot to the other, gazing across the rose garden, and the manicured lawn to where our Sunseeker is moored at the private jetty in the secluded part of the river.

It is the house he grew up in, under the glow of my privileged status; businessman, entrepreneur, executive, local benefactor, and almost politician.

His knuckles knead the palms of his hands as if he's washing them; spiritually cleansing. His small eyes are lost in his angular pallid face. His dark brows are knotted together as they were when he reappeared in our life a few months ago. He has been clean for two months and studying him now, I wonder how long he will stay in control before straying back down the dark path he vowed he would never walk again.

Frances paces the long length of the marble floor. Her hair is unkempt, ragged and unwashed. It is a reflection of her poor housing and her wasted life.

The IPhone I bought her is stuck to her ear. She is whispering but I hear every word. She is concerned about the Pole, as I called him. She has three year-old twins, Greta and Sascha, whom I have never seen. She flouted convention and everything we stood for. She went against her education, her religion and her teachings but she is my precious daughter. She is my flesh and blood.

Suzie reaches for another wad of tissues.

I have three days in this transient world with a foot in each camp. This life and the next. I am like the

Archangel Gabrielle but I bring no tidings of great joy unless the joy of saving three souls is joy.

There is no booming God's voice or a teasing Satan hiding over my shoulder. No pearly gates and no fiery hell - not so far. I am spoken to on another level, through my consciousness. It seeps into me what I must do. I am given this gift and I must choose before I transcend the human form in its entirety and become a spirit for ever - or depending on what you believe - a discarded heap of rotting bones.

My choice.

I can choose three to watch over and to care for on earth.

I will be a guardian angel but who will I choose?

Choose Barrabas! Save Barrabas! Let him go free.

In my family home there are tears, recriminations, pain and loss. They love me. They miss me.

Oh no they don't!

'Boo!' I call out. I am the audience. 'Boo! He's behind you,' I call again, to my family but they don't turn around. They can't hear me. They are not attuned to death as others are. They do not sense a chill in the air.

I am nothing. A nobody. But at this moment I am the most powerful force in their room; in my room, in my house.

I leave. Wooosssh like an actress who gathers her skirt and storms off (exit stage right), tossing amber curls over her shoulder and a flicker of distain at the audience.

I am too distraught to stay.

One day dead.

Who will I guard over?

Whose guardian angel will I be?

Who will be deserving of me?

I swoop over houses, past chimneys and turrets, past church spires and ugly gargoyles who spit as I soar free into the air, unchained by rock and concrete, unhinged like an open swinging door.

I am a kite. Sky bound, higher and higher into the night and days, watching eclipses of the moon and shadows fall across the sun. I am on a quest. I am a pirate of the universe robbing the weak of their ills and filling their souls with hope and love.

I am the Robin Hood of the afterlife. The provider of miracles. The sixth sense. I am faith. The one who listens to the kneeling prayers of the children and the one who listens to the failing prayers of the dying. I am given a precious gift to use wisely. To donate to three lucky winners.

Who shall I choose?

It's like the Lotto. Lady Luck! But this time there is no financial gain and no monetary reward. I cannot travel back in time like Superman and undo the past, unravel the lies, the hurt and deceit. I can only travel forward into the future, offering succour, guidance and strength. Therein lies my power.

I am empowered to help those who help themselves. I am the force that pushes you up the impossible hill. The willpower that makes you hang on. I am the grit that keeps you going even though you have no strength, or hope or bad health.

In Africa where tummies are bloated with hunger. In Asia where fevers are rampant, and in

South America where misery and hardship are an everyday occurrence. In Iraq, Syria and Afghanistan where wars rage and families are destroyed. In Eastern Europe where children are raped, beaten and forced into prostitution; enduring emotional and physical abuse at home and abroad. Suffering in hospitals, death, dying and disease.

I can make a difference. I can watch over three.

This is an opportunity.

Was I ever chosen? Was I ever one of the three?

Did I ever have a guardian angel? My Aunt, my father, or grandmother?

I am drawn irrevocably to my home. To the safety and security of my life on earth. I float through my study, my lounge, my reading room, my television room, my bedroom, my bathroom. The mourners are leaving. My family are alone, it is early morning, dirty, empty glasses are on every worktop but no-one clears them away.

I was kind but I hear my son call me tight.

I was brave but my daughter says I was weak.

I was considerate but my wife believes me selfish.

Denied three times and not a cockerel in sight.

Never speak ill of the dead they say.

I hear them. I am the transparent air they breathe. I inhale their thoughts, read their lips and listen to their barbed words and their vocal betrayal. A priest! A priest! A kingdom for a priest to absolve these sinners or to cast them into the murky hell below - where perhaps I am doomed to rest for all eternity - my path illuminated by grains of temptation or is it fear or redemption?

Suzie's tears have dried. She moves robotically and places a reassuring hand on Ben's shoulder. He returns her touch with a quick smile. Frances watches them both with tired eyes from the kitchen table.

"You'll be okay now Mum," Ben says. "This is all yours. You can do what you want." He waves his arm around the kitchen his fingers pointing toward the stationary boat moored under the bright moon at the bottom of our garden.

"You'll be stronger now Mum." Frances envelopes her mother in a hug. "It will be easier. You can make the decisions."

"I'll look after you both. I promise." Suzie pulls them both into a group hug. "Let's get the autopsy over."

Two days dead.

My motionless corpse is on the slab. I am curious. I never imagined I was that fat, my jowls so heavy, my chest so hairy. I am bruised and bloated in death in this white, clean, sterilised room. It is exactly how I like things. My idea of heaven; organised, professional and experienced.

But when it is time to cut me open I leave.

I vanish. I rise above the building, over the rooftops, across the green park and the flowering trees I can no longer smell and the warm sunshine I cannot feel. My hour glass is running dry.

I can watch over three.

Who deserves me?

Who can I be gallant enough to defend; through reason, through good sense, through kindness, through life's ups and downs?

My office is in mourning. My efficient secretary,

too ugly for an affair, is dealing with my business partners, my legal team and my managers. I leave quickly. I left orders in place if anything were to happen. I covered all eventualities. Financially, neither my family, nor my associates, nor my investors will suffer. I checked and cross-checked every box.

I am meticulous.

Decisions.

For a man who made decisions and stuck by them, this is my test.

The hardest choice I must make.

Who to choose?

Which three people can I protect, cherish and help to succeed? To help them achieve their dreams. To become the people they want to be. To have the strength to survive and to be true to themselves without compromise but with kindness, compassion and understanding?

There are uniformed men at my front door.

Ben's face is ashen.

Frances's mouth is O-shaped.

Suzie is slumped across the kitchen table.

My memory is vague.

Ben was at home. We were celebrating. Frances said she was having another baby with the Pole. Suzie said she was leaving me. We were fighting.

The uniformed man suggests to them, Ben drugged me. Frances hit me. Suzie pushed me down the stairs.

I fly away up high.

The hour glass runs dry.

Three days dead.

Who do I watch over?

I vowed I would never go there. They live in a dingy apartment on the wrong side of town.

The Pole is a good man and I see him for the first time with my two grandchildren Greta and Sascha. They need me, so too will my third grandchild who is yet unborn into this complicated and troubled world.

Red Shoes
Part Two

I'm flustered when I arrive at the school. The hall is busy and parents are seating themselves in rows of chairs facing the stage. I've spent the past few hours trying to calm Matt's nerves. He says he has a sore throat.

"He'll be fine," Harry says.

We sit on plastic chairs.

"It didn't help that Jason was so awful," I reply. "He shouldn't have kicked Matt."

"He didn't mean it. They're just boys…"

"I don't care. You should have said something." I'm leaning forward, my handbag is trapped under my high heel, and my hair falls across my face.

"Jo?"

I recognise Gary's voice before I look up.

"Can I sit here?" He sits down.

I can't believe the gall of my ex-husband. Marilyn is with him and she nods at me. They haven't brought the baby - thank God. Harry looks at Gary but I ignore him. I want the nativity play to begin.

"You're looking well, Jo. Love the new haircut. Is there a new man in your life?" I stare straight ahead. Then I feel Harry's arm across my chest.

"Harry Templeton." His palm is held out. "My son Jason is in the same class as Matt and we live across the street."

Gary takes the outstretched hand and smirks. I push their hands apart.

"Too much information," I say to Harry, and I see his birthmark elongate under his eye.

The audience shuffle, sneeze and cough. Mr Rogers appears on stage. He's wearing a red bow tie and matching waistcoat.

"He looks very festive," Gary says, "Is he gay?"

Mr Rogers' voice is low and controlled. With a smile and wave of his hand the curtains part and the nativity begins, but his words are lost on me.

Modestman.

I think of what he's asked me to do and what he wants each night and I feel my cheeks flush. I'm pleased when the lights dim and Mary is visited on stage by the Archangel Gabriel.

"He's a prick," Gary whispers. He nods at Harry. "How could you sleep with him?"

"I'm not!"

Gary smothers a laugh and I smell stale coffee from his breath.

Harry's gaze burns my cheeks.

"That's not what Matt says," Gary whispers.

Mary and Joseph arrive at the Inn. Mr Rogers is standing at the side of the stage. He is deep in thought, concentrating and nodding encouragement to the children. He is stroking his cheek.

"I want Matt to come and live with us," Gary hisses, "We're a proper family."

"We'd have been a proper family if you hadn't left," I reply.

Harry nudges me with his knee, wanting us to be quiet. I nudge him back harder.

The shepherds come on stage and Matt is in his dark robes carrying a stuffed toy, a white baby lamb with black ears, he is shaking. There is a hollow bang as the other shepherd-boy drops his crook. The audience giggle as he picks it up. I see Jason, who is Joseph, laughing, his eyes are wet with mirthful tears.

Mr Rogers's hair flops over his forehead and he nods encouragingly.

"The tea towel makes Matt look like an Arab terrorist," Gary says aloud and Marilyn snorts a laugh.

Matt begins to sing, his voice is shaky. It's hard to hear him.

"He'd have more confidence if he lived with us." Somehow he's grabbed my arm and he squeezes my skin. It hurts. I can't breathe. My body is rigid. I want Matt to succeed. To finish the carol and when he does I breathe a sigh of relief, and Gary stops pinching me. The audience applaud.

When I look up Mr Rogers is staring at me.

Modestman has found my face in the audience and singled me out.

I know then that he knows exactly who I am. It's like telepathy. Harry digs me in the ribs with his elbow. He's beaming proudly.

"I've spoken with the lawyer." Gary is clapping. "It's just a matter of time before I prove you're an unfit mother."

My mouth is dry.

"Are you still drinking?" I feel his spittle on my cheek.

I'm claustrophobic. I stand and push past Harry's knees and make my way to the exit. I run, not knowing the way, turning corners in the unfamiliar corridors until I find an emergency door and fling it open. Outside, I lean back against the wall, my warm breath comes out like a stream of smoke and when I bend over and gasp for air I can feel the bricks from the wall poking against my legs, snagging my stocking.

Beside me the door bursts open.

"I knew it," Modestman says. He's standing illuminated in the halo light. "It is you."

My eyes fill with tears. I want to deny it but the words stick in my throat. We stare at each other. Then he moves toward me and takes my chin in his hand. He kisses me. His lips are soft and I feel his tongue inside my mouth. Then he pulls quickly away. I hear his breathing but I don't see him. My eyes are still shut. He disappears back inside the school, banging the door and leaving me in darkness.

I sense Harry's anger the minute I step back inside the school hall.

"Your behaviour is disgraceful," he says. "How could you run out like that?"

I'm looking around for Matt but I can't see him. Parents are milling about, talking, laughing, pushing past each other to shake hands and kiss cheeks.

I'm an outcast.

"Where did you go?" he says.

"I needed some fresh air." I see Gary and Marilyn chatting with a group at the back of the hall and I turn away. "Where are the boys?"

I watch as Mr Rogers approaches with Matt and Jason at his side.

"Didn't they do a good job?" he says.

Harry replies but I don't listen. I keep my eyes firmly on Matt who is gazing adoringly at Mr Rogers.

"Happy Christmas," Mr Rogers says, as we are leaving. When he holds out his hand I feel his fingers squeezing mine but I don't look into his eyes.

Harry drives us home and I am listening to Matt and Jason. They are giggling about Simon dropping his shepherd's crook. Their voices are filled with relief and exuberance. It's all over. At home, I pour milk for the boys and wine for me and Harry. I've thrown off my coat, and kicked my red shoes into the corner of the room. It's still early but I'm drained.

"Matt tells me the computer is playing up." Harry nods at the old PC in the corner of the kitchen where the boys are gathered.

"Yes, I'll probably get a new one in the sales after Christmas."

"I didn't expect Gary to look like that. His wife's a bit of all right though." We go into the lounge and Harry leans back on the sofa and yawns loudly.

"Mum, the computer's not working," Matt shouts from the kitchen.

I don't say anything. I flick on lamps and sit in the chair opposite Harry.

"Mr Rogers is a strange one," Harry says, "It's not many men who want to be with small children every day. I mean, it's a bit unusual - I'd have thought it was more of a woman's job. I'd probably be quite suspicious if he wasn't getting married next year…"

Jason calls out, "Dad, come and help."

I look at Harry. He's smiling.

"That's surprised you, hasn't it? Did you know

he's going out with Miss Taylor the singing teacher?"

I couldn't place Miss Taylor. Instead I think of Modestman's tongue inside my mouth.

"I'm going to the bathroom," I say.

Harry stands up at the same time. His arms go around my waist and his face is close to mine.

"You can't deny what you feel, Jo. You can't keep fighting me. I know you want me. You're just frightened. You have to let go. You have to trust me. You have every right to love again." He bends his head for a kiss but I push his shoulders away and run from the room, conscious that I've been running from men all evening.

In the bathroom, I run the water and brush my teeth, afterwards I scrape globs of toothpaste from the handle and place it in the mug. I pull old hairs from a matted brush and flush them down the toilet before combing my hair. I hear Matt's footsteps on the landing. He shouts something and he runs down the stairs again.

I hear Gary's words in my head, It's just a matter of time before I prove you're an unfit mother, and my hands begin to shake. I find an old lipstick amongst the dried up cosmetics in a small basket and decide I don't like the colour but it will do for now. I check my stocking. There's a small ladder from the school wall and a scratch on my skin.

I'm walking down the stairs when I hear Harry's voice. He sounds agitated.

"Well, you'll just have to do something else. It's not working either. Go up to your room or go into the lounge and put on the television."

When I go into the kitchen the boys look

chastised. The mood in the house has changed.

"What's happened?"

Matt and Jason push past me and Harry's face is one of pure rage.

"Go on," he shouts. He is shaking. Under his arm I see a laptop. "Close the door behind you."

I stand bewildered.

The door closes and we are left alone. Harry places the laptop on the table and I recognise the cracked lid. He opens it. Livejasmin.com springs to life.

"What's this?" He's trying to control his voice.

I look at the images flashing before me. I've seen them thousands of times, square boxes of semi-nude women, posturing and displaying themselves, tempting, teasing, cajoling, some erotic, some sad.

I walk over to the table and snap the lid shut.

"You haven't answered me."

"I don't have to."

"I think I'm owed an explanation. The boys nearly saw this. They couldn't get onto the PC, so Matt fetched this from your bedroom."

"Matt knows this laptop is mine. He knows not to touch it. Why did you ask him to get it?"

"I...I didn't."

"You did. Matt would never have thought of it."

"I just asked him where Mum's laptop was.. "

"You must have told him to go and get it."

"That's not the point. What is this filth? I deserve an explanation."

"No, Harry. You don't. Our sons are friends and we are neighbours, nothing more."

"Well, it's not as if I haven't tried. Are you

having sex on the internet? Are you having sex with women?"

"Harry, I'm not explaining anything. The only thing I will say is - is that it is none of your business."

"Do you think this is suitable for Matt? Is this the way to raise your son?"

"This has nothing to do with Matt…or with you. I think you'd better go."

Harry pushes back his shoulders. His sleepy eyes are alive with anger. "I think Jason will stop coming over here. I don't want my son to be influenced by any of this filthy porn. It's revolting. I thought you'd have known better." He goes to the door. "Come on Jason, we're going home." His face looks grey when he turns to me. "I expected more from you, Jo. I thought you were worth far more than this."

An hour later, after I've tucked Matt into bed, chatted about the nativity play and reassured him Jason would still be his friend, my mobile rings.

I am in the kitchen and on my third glass of wine, and I am tracing the jagged crack on the lid with my finger. I've decided to take a night off and my head is pounding.

It is an unknown number but I answer anyway.

"Hello."

"I wasn't sure you'd pick up." There's a pause. "Do you know who this is?"

I'd heard his voice on the stage earlier that evening. I can still feel the pressure of his soft lips and the taste of his kiss.

"Yes."

"I got your number from the school records. Do you know why I'm phoning you?"

I lean forward, rubbing my temple with a thumb.
"No."

"You can't guess?"

"No."

"Do you want to meet up with me?"

"No."

"Why?"

"I don't think it's a good idea." I close my eyes.

"Why?"

"You're a headmaster, figure it out yourself."

His laugh is deep and throaty. "Why don't you explain it to me…over a drink?"

I look at my high heels in the corner of the kitchen.

"No."

"I'm trying to be nice here."

I don't say anything.

"I spoke to Gary tonight, Matt's Dad…"

My ear is burning and I pull on the lobe.

"He was asking me all sorts of stuff about Matt's welfare and things like that. Does he have a hidden agenda?"

I say nothing.

"He's remarried hasn't he?"

"Yes."

"With a new baby."

"Yes." I lean back against the chair and fold an arm across my chest.

"He seemed to be suggesting that it would be better if Matt lived with them. Would you like to have a drink and we can talk about it?"

"No"

"He wants custody of Matt."

"I know." I lean forward and rest my head on my arm, on the table.

"I think he wants to prove you're an unfit mother."

"Yes."

"How about that drink?"

"No."

"I think it would be a good idea, Jo. May I call you Jo?"

"You normally call me lots of other things."

He laughs. "I think you need me on your side."

"Why?" I sit up straight.

"Well, Gary wouldn't want to find out about you, would he?"

"And the school wouldn't want to find out about you, either."

"You can't prove anything, Jo."

"Neither can you,"

"Yes I can. I've made copies."

I play with the laptop and finger the plastic crack. I feel my skin opening, just a small cut, a paper cut, but it is painful and I suck the blood.

"So? How about that drink?"

"Okay," I say.

"It sounds like you're sucking your finger.

I say nothing.

"Are you?"

"Yes."

"Go online," he says. "I want to see you."

I say nothing.

"Hurry up!"

COMING SOON...

MASTERPIECE by Janet Pywell

The Golden Icon is the first in a trilogy following the quest of opera singer Josephine Lavelle.

In the second novel, Masterpiece, Josephine is recovering from a bullet wound to her lung. She begins her journey, to find her adopted child, in London where she gave birth almost thirty years ago Her trek takes her back to Ireland and to Spain as she becomes embroiled in the death of a friend, and a stolen painting of Vermeer's - The Concert – thought to be the most valuable un-recovered, stolen painting in the world.

Followed by her arch enemy, journalist Karl Blakey, she is plunged into a foreign world of forgers, dealers and double crossers but Josephine is determined to save her child – but at what price?

Will Josephine have to make the ultimate sacrifice to make amends for her past secret?

ABOUT THE AUTHOR

Janet Pywell believes that her experience of living and travelling abroad has been invaluable, adding perspective and depth to her writing to help plot stories and create fictional characters.

With a background in travel and tourism, Janet has worked in administration and sales before becoming Director of her own marketing company. Pursuing her dream to write Janet studied with the Open University and at Queen's University Belfast. She holds an MA in Creative Writing.

Red Shoes and Other Short Stories are a testament to Janet's defence, to travel frequently and widely, with the excuse of gathering book fodder for her writing.

The Golden Icon, Janet's debut novel is the first of a trilogy.

5119890R00103

Printed in Great Britain
by Amazon.co.uk, Ltd.,
Marston Gate.